Minnie

Minnie

Annie M. G. Schmidt

Translated from the Dutch by Lance Salway

Illustrated by Kay Sather

MILKWEED
EDITIONS

Publication of Minnie is made possible in part by a gift from the Lawrence M. and Elizabeth Ann O'Shaughnessy Charitable Income Trust in honor of Lawrence M. O'Shaughnessy.

Printed in the United States of America
Design by Don Leeper. Typeset in Goudy by Stanton Publication Services.
94 95 96 97 98   5 4 3 2

Milkweed Editions is supported by the Elmer and Eleanor Andersen Foundation; Dayton Hudson Foundation for Dayton's and Target Stores; Ecolab Foundation; General Mills Foundation; Honeywell Foundation; Jerome Foundation; John S. and James L. Knight Foundation; The McKnight Foundation; Andrew W. Mellon Foundation; Minnesota State Arts Board through an appropriation by the Minnesota State Legislature; Musser Fund; Literature and Challenge Programs of the National Endowment for the Arts; I. A. O'Shaughnessy Foundation; Piper Family Fund of the Minneapolis Foundation; Piper Jaffray Companies, Inc.; John and Beverly Rollwagen Fund; Star Tribune/Cowles Media Foundation; Surdna Foundation; James R. Thorpe Foundation; Unity Avenue Foundation; Lila Wallace-Reader's Digest Literary Publishers Marketing Development Program, funded through a grant to the Council of Literary Magazines and Presses; and generous individuals.

Library of Congress Cataloging-in-Publication Data

Schmidt, Annie M.G.
    [Minoes. English]
    Minnie / Annie M.G. Schmidt ; translated from the Dutch by Lance Salway. — 1st ed.
        p. cm.
    "First published in 1970 in the Netherlands under the title Minoes"—T.p. verso.
    Summary: Minnie, formerly a cat but now a woman with many cattish ways, helps Tibbs, a newspaper reporter, with information she gets from her many feline friends.
    ISBN 1-57131-601-9 (hc)—1-57131-600-0 (pbk)
    [1. Cats—Fiction.   2. Reporters and reporting—Fiction.]   I. Title
PZ7.S3497Mi 1994
[Fic]—dc20

                                                        93-35924
                                                        CIP
                                                        AC

Contents

Minnie

Chapter 1

Looking for News

"Tibbs! Where is Tibbs! Has anyone seen Tibbs? The boss wants him. Where on earth is he? *Tibbs!*"

Tibbs could hear what they were saying perfectly well. But he stayed hidden behind his desk. And he trembled as he thought to himself: I don't want to go and see the boss. I don't dare. I know exactly what's going to happen. This time I really *am* going to get fired.

"Tibbs! Ah, there you are!"

Now he was in for it. They'd found him.

"You've got to go and see the boss right away, Tibbs."

There was no getting out of it now. He would have to go. And so, with head bowed, Tibbs walked down the corridor and stopped outside a door marked *Editor*.

He knocked. A voice said, "Yes?"

When Tibbs walked in, his boss was busy on the telephone. He pointed to a chair and carried on with his conversation.

Tibbs sat down and waited.

These were the offices of the *Chillthorn Courier*. Tibbs had a job with this newspaper. He was a reporter.

"Now then," said the editor as he put down the receiver.

"I want to have a serious talk with you, Tibbs."

Here it comes, Tibbs thought.

"The stories you write are very nice, Tibbs. Sometimes they're very nice indeed."

Tibbs smiled. Perhaps it was going to be all right, after all.

"But . . ."

Tibbs waited patiently. There had to be a *but*, of course. He wouldn't be here otherwise.

"But they don't say anything *new*. I've told you this often enough before now. Your stories are always about cats."

Tibbs said nothing. It was true. He was extremely fond of cats. He knew all the cats in the neighborhood. He even had one himself.

"But I wrote an article yesterday that had nothing to do with cats," he said. "It was about spring."

"Exactly," said the editor. "About spring. About leaves coming out on the trees again. Do you call that *news?*"

"Well, they were *new* leaves," said Tibbs.

The editor sighed. "Now listen to me carefully, Tibbs," he said. "I like you. You're a good guy and you write nice little stories. But we're working on a newspaper here. And a newspaper must have news."

"But there's so much news in the paper already," said Tibbs. "Wars and things. And murders. I just thought that it would be nice for people to read something about cats and leaves for a change."

"No, Tibbs. Don't get me wrong, I'm not asking you to write about murders or bank robberies. But a town like ours is full of little news stories. If you know where to find them. But, as I've told you often enough before, you're much too shy. You're too scared to interview people. You don't have the courage to ask questions. It seems to me that you only feel really at home with cats."

Again Tibbs said nothing, because it was true. He *was* shy. And this is the last thing you should be if you work on a newspaper. You have to be prepared to interview anyone. You have to be prepared to interview the pastor—when he's in the bath if necessary. And ask him confidently, "Tell me now, what have you been doing tonight?"

A good newspaperman can do all this. But not Tibbs.

"Now then," said the editor. "I'll give you *one* more chance. From now on you must only write articles that have news in them. I want to see the first one tomorrow afternoon. And I want to see a few more after that during the week. And if you can't manage it . . ."

Tibbs knew what he was going to say. He would lose his job.

"Have a good day, Tibbs."

"You too, sir."

Tibbs went outside, into the street. It was raining gently and everything looked gray. Tibbs wandered through the town. He looked around him as he walked, noticing everything that was going on. Where on earth was he going to find some news?

He saw cars. Cars that were being driven and cars that were parked. He saw a few pedestrians and here and there a cat. But he couldn't write about cats anymore. He began to feel tired after a while and sat down on a bench in Market Square, under a tree where it was still dry.

Someone was already sitting on the bench. Tibbs saw at once who it was. It was his old teacher from school, Mr. Smith.

"Well, fancy meeting you!" said Mr. Smith. "How nice to see you again. I hear that you're working for the paper now. I always thought that you'd work for a newspaper one day. It's all going well, I take it?"

Tibbs swallowed hard and said, "Oh yes, very well."

"You always used to write such beautiful essays at school," said Mr. Smith. "I knew that you'd go far. Oh yes, you write very well indeed."

"Tell me something I don't know," Tibbs said.

Mr. Smith looked offended. "You're very full of yourself, aren't you?" he asked. "All I said was that you write very well and you asked me to tell you something you don't know. That's not very polite, is it?"

"I didn't mean it like that," said Tibbs, going red. He started to explain what he *did* mean, but then he stopped. There was a sudden angry barking close by. They both looked up. A large German shepherd raced past them, chasing something. They couldn't quite see what the *something* was. It disappeared between the parked cars, and the dog dashed after it. Immediately afterwards there was a loud rustling in a tall elm tree nearby.

"A cat," said Mr. Smith. "A cat's climbed the tree."

"Are you sure it was a cat?" asked Tibbs. "It was so big. And it seemed to flutter. It looked more like a large bird. A stork or something like that."

"Storks don't run," said Mr. Smith.

"No, but they *do* flutter. I've never heard of a cat fluttering."

They went to have a look.

The dog was standing beneath the tree, barking angrily.

They tried to see if there was anything in the branches. But the cat was completely hidden. If it *was* a cat.

[4]

"Come here, Mars!" The dog was being called. "*Mars!* Here!"

A man came up, carrying a dog leash. He fastened the leash to the collar and began to pull.

"Grrr!" said Mars. He was dragged unwillingly away across the pavement.

And then they saw something, high above them among the new leaves.

A leg. A leg wearing an elegant sock and a shiny leather shoe.

"Good heavens, it's a woman," said Mr. Smith.

"How did she get up there?" said Tibbs. "It's so high. How on earth did she get up the tree so quickly?"

And then a face appeared. A worried face with big frightened eyes and a mass of ginger hair.

"Has he gone?" the face called.

"Yes, he's gone," Tibbs called back. "Come on down!"

"I can't," the woman wailed. "It's too high."

Tibbs looked around. A delivery van was parked close by. He climbed carefully onto the roof of the van and reached up as far as he could. The woman started to crawl on all fours to the end of a branch. Then she dropped onto a lower branch and grasped Tibbs's hand.

She seemed extremely agile. With one jump she landed on the roof of the van and then another hop brought her to the ground.

"I dropped my case," she said. "Can you see it anywhere?"

It was lying in the gutter. Mr. Smith picked it up.

"Here you are," he said. "Your clothes are a bit dirty."

The young woman brushed dust and leaves from her dress and said, "It was such a big dog. I couldn't help it. I just have to climb a tree whenever I see a dog. Thank you very much indeed."

Tibbs decided that he would ask her some questions. He had just remembered his article and this would at least be something different to write about.

But he hesitated a little too long. He was too shy as usual. By the time he had plucked up his courage, the young woman had gone off with her suitcase.

"What a curious woman," said Mr. Smith. "She looks just like a cat."

"Yes," said Tibbs. "She does look amazingly like a cat."

They watched as she disappeared around a corner.

I'll catch up with her, thought Tibbs. He left Mr. Smith behind without saying so much as a good-bye and ran down the street after the young woman. There she was in front of him. He would say to her: "Excuse me, madam, why are you so frightened of dogs and how can you climb trees so quickly?"

And then, all of a sudden, he lost sight of her.

Had she gone inside one of the houses? But there were no doors on that part of the street. Just a stretch of fence with a garden behind. And there was no gate in the fence; she must have crept between the boards. Tibbs peered through the fence into a garden. He could see a lawn and bushes. But no young woman.

"Oh, she's probably gone in through a door somewhere," Tibbs said to himself. "I must have just missed her. And it's beginning to rain harder now. I'm going home."

On the way he bought two fish fillets and a bag of pears for supper. Tibbs lived in an attic. It was a very nice attic with one big room where he lived and slept. There was also a small kitchen, a bathroom and a storeroom. He had to climb a great many stairs to get there but once he was at the top he could look out across a mass of rooftops and chimneys. His big gray cat Fluff sat waiting for him.

"You can smell the fillets," said Tibbs. "Come into the kitchen and we'll cook the fish and eat them. You can have a whole one, Fluff. This may be the last time I'll be able to buy fish. Because I'm going to get fired tomorrow. I'll have had it, Fluff. I won't be earning anything at all. Then we'll have to go out begging together."

"Miaow," said Fluff.

"*Unless* I can find some news to write about this evening," said Tibbs. "But it's too late for that now."

He sliced some bread and made a pot of tea. He ate in

the kitchen, together with Fluff. And then he went to sit in the living room, behind his typewriter.

Perhaps I should try and write something about that strange young woman, he thought.

And he began:

> *At about five o'clock this afternoon, a young woman was chased by a German shepherd in Market Square. In her panic, she climbed right to the top of one of the tall elm trees. Seeing that she did not dare to come down, I offered her a helping hand, after which she went on her way and crept into the garden through a gap in the fence.*

Tibbs read it through. It was only a very short article. And he had a feeling that his boss would say, "Not *another* story about cats."

Better try again, thought Tibbs. I'll have a peppermint first, though. Then I'll be able to work better.

He searched his desk for the roll of peppermints. Oh no, I thought I had some here. "Do you know where I left the peppermints, Fluff?"

"Miaow," said Fluff.

"So you don't know either. What's the matter, do you want to go out? Surely you don't need to go out on the roof again?"

Tibbs opened the kitchen window and Fluff disappeared into the darkness.

It was still raining gently and a gust of cold wind blew inside.

Tibbs went back to the typewriter. He inserted a fresh sheet of paper and began again.

Chapter 2

A Stray Cat

While Tibbs sat brooding in his attic, the strange young woman was not very far away.

She was sitting in a garden a few streets further on, hidden among the bushes. It was night now and pitch dark. A wind was blowing and the garden was very wet.

She sat there for a while with her suitcase. Then she made a tiny mewing sound. Nothing happened at first.

She made the noise once again. And then an answer came from the direction of the house.

"Miaow . . ."

A very old and dignified black cat came slowly towards her. She stopped suspiciously a short distance from the bushes.

"Aunt Molly," the young woman whispered.

The old cat spat and backed away.

"I can see who it is now," she hissed. "*You!*"

"So you recognize me, Aunt Molly?"

"You're Minnie. My niece Minnie from Queen's Road."

"Yes, auntie. I heard you were living here and so I thought I'd drop in."

"I heard all about it," the old cat said nervously. "I heard what happened to you. All the cats are talking about it. How on earth did it happen, Minnie? To you of all people, from one of the finest cat families in Chillthorn! What did the rest of the family have to say about it?"

"They won't have anything more to do with me," said the young woman. "They say that it must have been my own fault. My sister even turned her tail up at me."

"Ssss," said Aunt Molly. "I don't blame her. You must have done something really terrible to be punished so. To be turned into a human! What a dreadful punishment! I wouldn't be a human for a thousand canaries. Tell me one thing, though, did witchcraft have anything to do with it?"

"I don't know," said Minnie.

"But surely you must know how it happened?"

"All I know is that I went out one day as a cat and came back as a woman."

"I just can't believe it," said Aunt Molly. "You must have done something to deserve it. You probably did something very uncattish. What was it?"

"Nothing. I didn't do anything, as far as I know."

"And you're wearing clothes," Aunt Molly went on. "Where did they come from?"

"I—I took them," the young woman said. "I couldn't walk around naked, could I?"

"Bah! And a suitcase too," hissed Aunt Molly. "Where did you get that?"

"I took it as well."

"What's in it?"

"Night things. And a toothbrush. And a washcloth and soap."

"Don't you wash yourself with spit anymore?"

"No."

[11]

"Then all is lost!" said Aunt Molly. "I had hoped that you would soon get back to normal but now I fear there's no hope for you."

"Aunt Molly, I'm hungry. Do you have anything for me to eat?"

"I'm sorry but I've nothing at all. I've finished my supper for the evening. And my human is very fussy. She never leaves food lying about. Everything goes straight into the fridge."

"Is she nice?" asked Minnie.

"I suppose so. Why?"

"Would she like me to live here too?"

"*No!*" cried Aunt Molly in alarm. "What an idea, child! The way you are now!"

"I'm looking for somewhere to live, Aunt Molly. I must find shelter somewhere. Do you know where I could go? Somewhere nearby?"

"I'm old," said Aunt Molly. "I hardly ever go out on to the rooftops anymore and very seldom into another garden. But I still have a few friends. The cat of Mr. Smith the teacher lives in the next garden. In that direction. Go and talk to him. The cat's name is Simon. Cross-Eyed Simon. He's a Siamese but very pleasant even so."

"And would I be able to stay—"

"No, no," said Aunt Molly. "You wouldn't be able to stay there either. But Simon knows all the cats around here. And so he knows all the people too. If anyone can help you, he can."

"Thank you very much, Aunt Molly. Good-bye then. I'll drop in again one of these days."

"If you don't have any luck," said her aunt, "then have a

talk with the Scruffy Cat. She's a stray. You can usually find her on the roof of the Building Society. Not that she has much of a reputation, she's nothing but a tramp. But she does know a great deal because she wanders around the whole town."

"Thanks."

"And now I'm going indoors," said Aunt Molly. "I feel extremely sorry for you but I still say that you have only yourself to blame. Just one word of advice: do try and wash yourself with spit. That is the beginning and end of all wisdom."

With her tail held high, Aunt Molly walked away across the garden toward the house. Her poor niece picked up her suitcase and crept through a hole in the hedge. In search of the cat next door.

Tibbs was having a very bad time of it. He walked anxiously up and down his room. Every now and then he sat down at his typewriter but soon he tore up what he'd written and got up again. He rummaged in all the drawers of his desk in search of his peppermints, because he had got the idea into his head that he couldn't think properly without them. And all the time it was getting later and later.

"At this rate I'll just have to go out again," he said. "To see if anything's happening there that I can write about. But I don't expect anyone will be outside in this weather. It's odd that Fluff has stayed out on the roof for such a long time. He usually comes back sooner than this. I may as well go to bed, I suppose. I'll go and see the boss tomorrow. And I'll say: 'I'm sorry, you're right, I'm no use to the paper.' And then he'll say: 'All right, then. It seems to me that it will be best if you look for something else.' And that will be that. I'll go off and find another job."

There was a sudden sound from the kitchen.

The garbage can.

"That'll be Fluff," Tibbs said to himself. "The little devil! He's trying to get the fish bones from the garbage can. And he's already had a whole fillet. I'd better go and have a look before he upsets the can completely. I'll only have to sweep everything up."

Tibbs stood up and opened the kitchen door.

And he nearly jumped out of his skin.

It wasn't Fluff. It was a young woman. The young woman from the tree. And she was busy rummaging through his garbage can. There was only one way she could have got in—through the skylight.

She turned around as soon as she heard him. She had a big fish bone in her mouth. She looked so much like a timid wet stray cat that Tibbs had to stop himself from shouting, "Scat! Be off with you!" But he didn't say anything.

She took the bone out of her mouth and gave him a friendly smile. She had slightly slanting green eyes.

"Please forgive me," she said. "I was sitting on the roof with your cat, Fluff. And the smell was so wonderful. So I climbed in through the skylight. He's still outside."

She was very elegant and well-spoken. But she was wet through. Her red hair hung in dank wisps around her face and her dress was soaking and crumpled. He suddenly felt very sorry for her.

She was like a pathetic half-drowned cat. A stray cat!

"I'm afraid we finished the fish," said Tibbs. "But if you're hungry, I can let you have a sau—" He almost said a saucer of milk. "A *glass* of milk. And a sandwich, perhaps? With sardines?"

"Thank you very much," she said politely. She looked as though she might faint with hunger at any moment.

"Then you'd better put *that* back," said Tibbs, pointing at the fish bone she was still holding in her hand.

She threw the bone in the garbage can. And then she sat down timidly and damply on the kitchen chair to watch Tibbs opening a tin of sardines.

"May I know your name?" Tibbs asked.

"Minnie. Miss Minnie."

"And I'm—"

"Mr. Tibbs," she said. "I already know."

"Just call me Tibbs. Everyone calls me Tibbs."

"I'd rather call you *Mr.* Tibbs if you don't mind."

"What were you doing on the roof?" he asked.

"I—er—I was looking for a job."

Tibbs looked at her in amazement. "On the roof?"

But she didn't answer. The sandwiches were ready. Tibbs was about to put the plate on the floor but stopped himself just in time. She probably eats just like a normal person, he thought. And he was right. She ate the sandwiches very daintily with her fingers.

"You've got a job on the newspaper," she said between bites. "But not for much longer."

"How on earth do you know that?" Tibbs cried.

"Someone told me," she said. "The article isn't working out. The article about me in the tree. Pity."

"What do you mean, someone told you?" said Tibbs. "I'd really like to know how you found out. *I* haven't said a word to anyone."

He waited until she had finished eating. She took the last bite. Then she picked the crumbs from the plate with her finger and then licked the finger.

Then her eyes began to close.

She's falling asleep, thought Tibbs.

But she wasn't asleep. She was staring contentedly in front of her. And then Tibbs heard a soft rumbling sound. The young woman was purring.

"I asked you a question," said Tibbs.

"Oh, yes," she said. "I just heard someone talking about it."

Tibbs sighed. Then he noticed that she was shivering. No wonder, in all those wet clothes.

"Haven't you anything dry to put on?"

"Yes," she said. "In my suitcase."

It was then Tibbs noticed that she had a suitcase with her. It was standing under the windowsill.

"You must have a hot shower," he said. "And change into something dry. Otherwise you'll be ill tomorrow. The bathroom is over there."

"Thank you very much," she said. She picked up the suitcase and got up to go. And then, as she walked past him, she rubbed her head against his sleeve.

She wants to be stroked! Tibbs thought. He backed quickly away as if he had been touched by a crocodile.

When she had disappeared into the bathroom, Tibbs went and sat down in the living room. "I must be dreaming!" he said to himself. "A strange woman comes through my skylight. Starving. Who purrs and asks to be stroked."

Suddenly he had a dreadful thought. Surely she didn't—surely she didn't want to come and live with him? She had

said that she was looking for a job. But it was obvious that she was really looking for somewhere to live. A stray cat.

"I won't allow it," said Tibbs. "I already have a cat. I'm very happy living on my own and being my own boss. And I've only got one bed, anyway. How stupid of me to let her have a shower here."

There she was again. She came into the living room.

I knew it, Tibbs thought. What did I tell you? She was wearing a dressing gown and pajamas, with a pair of slippers on her feet.

She pointed to the wet dress that she was carrying over one arm. "May I dry this by the fire, please?"

"Er—yes, of course," said Tibbs. "But I'd just like to say right away—"

"What?"

"Look, you're welcome to wait here until your clothes are dry. But you can't *stay* here."

"Oh."

"No. I'm sorry. But it's quite out of the question."

"Oh," she said. "Not even for one night?"

"No," said Tibbs. "I don't have a spare bed."

"I don't need a bed. There's a big empty box in the store-room. A cardboard box that used to have cans of soup in it."

"A box?" asked Tibbs. "You want to sleep in a box?"

"Yes. If you'd just put some clean newspaper inside first."

Tibbs shook his head firmly. "I'll give you some money for a hotel," he said. "There's one quite close by."

He reached for his wallet but she waved it away at once. "Oh no," she said. "There's no need. If it isn't possible then I'll just leave. I'll put my wet dress on again and go at once."

She looked so forlorn. And she seemed so anxious. And

he could hear the wind and the rain outside. He couldn't send a poor cat out into the night in this weather.

"All right, then, just for *one* night," said Tibbs.

"May I have the box?"

"Of course. But on one condition. I want to know who told you so much about me. Who I am and where I work and the article I'm trying to write."

They heard a thud in the kitchen. Fluff had come back at last from his journey across the rooftops. His gray fur was wet.

"I learned everything from him," said Miss Minnie. And she pointed at Fluff. "He told me all about you. In fact, I've spoken to lots of cats in the neighborhood and they all say how nice you are."

Tibbs went red. Flattery only made him feel embarrassed. "You—you talk to cats?" he asked.

"Yes."

What nonsense, thought Tibbs. She must be out of her mind.

"And—er—why are you able to talk to cats?"

"I used to be one myself," she said.

Mad as a hatter, thought Tibbs.

Miss Minnie had sat down by the fire beside Fluff. They sat side by side on the hearthrug and Tibbs could hear them both purring. It sounded very peaceful. Perhaps I should get back to my article about her, Tibbs thought.

Tonight I gave shelter to a purring young woman who came into my house through the skylight and, in answer to my questions, informed me that she used to be a cat . . .

Then I really would be thrown out on my ear, thought Tibbs. He could hear them talking to each other, the young woman and the cat. They were making little mewing noises.

"What's Fluff telling you now?" he asked by way of a joke.

"He says that your peppermints are in a jam jar on the top shelf of the bookcase. You put them there yourself."

Tibbs got up to look. She was right.

Chapter 3

The Scruffy Cat

"I still can't believe it," said Tibbs. "I still can't believe that you can really talk to cats. You must be imagining it. It's some kind of mind reading or something."

"Perhaps," Miss Minnie said dreamily. She yawned. "I'm going into my box," she said. "May I take this old newspaper with me?"

"Are you quite sure that you don't want a blanket or a pillow?"

"Oh no, I don't need them at all. I believe that Fluff likes to sleep on your feet. We all have our particular preferences, you see. Sleep well."

"Good night, Miss Minnie."

When she reached the door, she turned around. "I heard some news on my way here," she said. "On the roof somewhere."

"News? What sort of news?"

"The Scruffy Cat is going to have some more kittens soon."

"Oh?" said Tibbs. "I'm not allowed to write about cats anymore. They don't think it's interesting enough."

"That's a pity," said Miss Minnie.

"Did you hear any other news?"

"Just that Mr. Smith is feeling very sorry for himself."

"Mr. Smith? Do you mean the teacher? I was talking to him only today. The two of us helped you out of the tree. He didn't look at all sad to me."

"But he is."

"It's not very interesting news, though," said Tibbs. "Is he in a bad mood or something?"

"In a week's time he will have been headmaster of the school for twenty-five years," said Miss Minnie. "He was hoping that there'd be a special celebration. An anniversary party. But no."

"Why isn't there going to be a party?"

"Because no one knows about it. Everyone has forgotten. He thought that people would remember but no one has given it a thought."

"Couldn't he remind them himself?"

"He won't do that. He's much too obstinate. That's what Cross-Eyed Simon says, anyway."

"Cross-Eyed Simon? That's his Siamese cat."

"Exactly. I've spoken to him. And he told me all about it. And now I'm going into my box."

She gave Fluff another "Miaow." And Fluff said "Miaow" back. This obviously meant: "Sleep well."

Tibbs picked up the telephone directory. It was getting very late but he dialed Mr. Smith's number just the same.

"I hope you don't mind me calling you so late," Tibbs said quickly. "But I've only just heard that you're going to be celebrating an anniversary. You've been headmaster for twenty-five years. Is that right?"

There was silence for a long time at the other end. And then Mr. Smith said, "So someone *has* remembered, after all."

Tibbs was about to say that it was the cats who had remembered but he stopped himself.

"Of course," he said enthusiastically. "How could anyone forget? I hope you'll have no objection to me writing an article about you?"

"I would be honored," said Mr. Smith.

"May I come and talk to you about it? It is awfully late, I know, but I would like to hand the article in tomorrow. Just something about your life and about the school—"

"Come on over," said Mr. Smith.

It was three o'clock in the morning when Tibbs came home. His notebook was full of facts about the life and work of Mr. Smith. Before sitting down at his typewriter, he peered into the storeroom.

The young woman lay curled up in the box. She was asleep.

She's saved me, thought Tibbs. I've got a story at last. All I have to do now is write it.

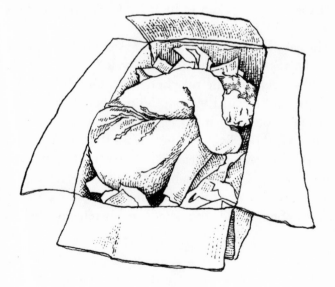

When at last he went to bed he said to Fluff, "I'll hand it in tomorrow. It's a good story. And it's real news."

Fluff came and lay down on his feet and went back to sleep.

I'll thank that strange Minnie tomorrow morning, Tibbs thought, and he fell asleep too.

But when he got up the next morning she had gone.

The box was empty. There was fresh newspaper inside and everything was clean and tidy. But there were no clothes and no suitcase.

"Did she say anything before she went, Fluff?"

"Miaow," said Fluff. But Tibbs didn't understand him.

"Well," he said, "I'm quite relieved really. The attic is all mine again now."

Then he saw the article lying on the desk. "How marvelous!" he cried. "I can go to the newspaper and say that I've got some news at last. I won't get fired after all. Well, not today, anyway." The happiness vanished. When evening came he would have to wander around the town all over again.

There was a smell of coffee. He went into the kitchen and saw that coffee had been made for him. And the dishes had been washed. That was kind of her.

The skylight was open. The stray had gone out through the skylight.

It's a good thing the weather's improved, thought Tibbs. She won't have to roam about in the rain. I wonder if she'll talk to the cats again? If she'd stayed here, he thought, *if* I'd taken her in, then perhaps she would have found some news for me every day. He wanted to run to the window and shout across the rooftops: "Puss, puss, puss! Minnie!"

But he didn't. "Now, don't be so selfish," he told himself.

"You only want her back out of self-interest. What a nasty character you are! Forget about her and find some news on your own. Don't be so shy. Anyway, she's gone for good now. She's probably miles away by now."

But Miss Minnie was very close by, as it happened. She was sitting on the roof of the Building Society, the highest roof in the neighborhood. She was talking to the Scruffy Cat.

The Scruffy Cat had been given her name because she was grubby and bedraggled and usually had muddy paws. Her tail was thin and skinny. There was a chunk out of her left ear. And her straggly fur was dingy and drab.

"You're going to have kittens soon," said Miss Minnie.

"Don't remind me," said the Scruffy Cat. "Sometimes I wonder if there'll ever be an end to it. Life is just one darned litter after another."

"How many kittens have you had so far?" asked Minnie.

The Scruffy Cat had a good scratch. "Damned if I know," she said. She always used very bad language. But that's what happens when you're a stray cat. "Anyway, let's not talk about me," she went on. "You're in a much worse state than I am. How did it happen? What on earth went wrong?"

She looked at Minnie with anxious yellow eyes.

"If only I knew. And do you know what the worst thing is? Not being a *complete* human being but only half of one."

"But you *are* a complete human. From top to bottom."

"I mean *inside*," said Minnie. "I still feel like a real cat. I purr, I hiss, I like to be stroked. Mind you, I do wash with a washcloth. I wonder if I still like mice? I must try one and see."

"Do you still know the Great Miaow-Miaow Song?" the Scruffy Cat asked.

"I think so."

"Sing a couple of bars then."

Minnie opened her mouth. A ghastly raucous caterwaul came out, a deafening screech that was loud enough to wake the dead.

The Scruffy Cat immediately joined in and together they screamed as loudly as they could. They carried on until a nearby window opened and a big empty bottle came flying out at them. The bottle smashed in pieces on the roof.

"That's got them going!" the Scruffy Cat cried happily. "Can I tell you something? It's going to pass. You'll be all right again. Anyone who can sing as well as that will always be a cat. Feel your upper lip. Are there any whiskers there?"

Minnie felt. "No," she said.

"And what about your tail? What's happened to that?"

"Gone completely."

"Do you ever feel that it might come back again?"

"Of course. But there's no sign of it yet. Not even the smallest little bump."

"Have you got a home?" asked the Scruffy Cat.

"I think I may have—but I'm not sure if it's going to work out."

"With the young man from the newspaper?"

"Yes," said Minnie. "I'm still hoping that he'll call me back in. I've left my suitcase over there, in the gutter behind the chimney."

"You'd be much better off as a stray," said the Scruffy Cat. "It's really nice being a stray. Come along with me. I'll introduce you to some of my children. Most of my children have done all right for themselves. One of my sons is the Canteen Cat at the factory. And one of my daughters is the Council Cat. She lives in the City Hall. And then there's—"

"Sssh—quiet a minute," said Minnie.

They fell silent. Across the rooftop came a voice: "Puss, puss, puss, puss! Minnie!"

"There you are," said Minnie. "He's calling me."

"Don't go," hissed the Scruffy Cat. "Stay a stray. Be free! Before you know where you are he'll be taking you to the vet in a basket. For an injection!"

Minnie hesitated. "I still think I ought to go," she said.

"You're a fool," said the Scruffy Cat. "Come along with me. I know an old trailer over at the parking lot. You could take shelter there. You could become a cat again in your own time."

"Puss, puss, puss! Minnie!"

"I'm going," said Minnie.

"No, stay here! Think about it. If you have any kittens, they'll all be drowned!"

"Puss, puss! *Miss* Minnie!" called the voice.

"I'll come and see you again," said Miss Minnie. "Here on the roof. Good-bye."

She jumped onto a lower roof. Then she climbed nimbly up a steep tiled roof and dropped down on the other side. Then she crawled on all fours along the gutter, picked up her suitcase and ended up soon afterwards by the kitchen window.

"Here I am," she said.

"Come on in," said Tibbs.

Chapter 4

The Cats' Press Agency

"Sit down, Tibbs," said the editor.

Tibbs sat down. It was exactly a week since he had last sat in that chair, blinking in the light. That had been a very unpleasant conversation. It was very different this time.

"I don't know what's come over you," the editor said. "But you've really changed, Tibbs. I was on the point of kicking you out last week, do you know that? I wanted to fire you, once and for all. Still, I expect you realized that. Then I decided to give you one more chance. And just look what's happened! In one week you've trotted out any number of interesting news stories. You were the first to hear about Mr. Smith and his anniversary. And you were the first person to know anything about the new swimming pool. It was highly confidential but you *still* got to hear about it. I wish I knew how you found out!"

"That would be telling," said Tibbs. "I'm afraid I can't reveal my sources."

These "sources" happened to be Minnie. And Minnie had heard about it from the Council Cat, who sat in on all the confidential Council meetings at City Hall.

"And that story about the discovery at the church," said the editor. "The pot of old coins they found in the church-yard. You were the first on the scene as usual."

Tibbs gave a modest smile. One of the Scruffy Cat's daughters had brought him that particular piece of news. Cassock the Church Cat. And it was she herself who had found the pot of old coins when she was digging a hole in the churchyard for the usual reason that cats dig holes. Tibbs had gone straight to the church to get all the details. And he had written a story about it right afterwards.

"Keep up the good work," said the editor. "You've obviously quite got over your shyness now."

Tibbs went red. This wasn't true, alas. He was just as shy as before. The news stories came from the cats and all he had to do was write them down. Mind you, he often had to check whether everything the cats had told him was true. But a single telephone call was usually all that was needed: "Excuse me, sir, but I just happen to have heard this or that and so and so. Is it true?" And everything *had* been true so far. The cats hadn't lied to him.

And there were an awful lot of cats in Chillthorn. Every building had at least one. There was even a cat sitting on the windowsill of the editor's office at that very moment.

It was the Newspaper Cat. He winked at Tibbs.

That cat listens to everything, Tibbs thought. I hope he doesn't say nasty things about me.

"I've been thinking things over," said the editor, "and I've decided to raise your salary at the end of the month."

"Thank you very much indeed," said Tibbs. "That's extremely kind of you, sir." He sneaked a look at the News-paper Cat and felt his face going red again. The cat seemed to be looking at him with contempt. He was probably

[31]

thinking that Tibbs was being much too humble.

Tibbs was so excited that when he got outside into the sunshine once more he felt like jumping up and down. Instead he shouted a loud "Hello" as he saw a familiar face coming towards him.

It was Bibi, a small girl who lived nearby and sometimes came to visit him.

"Would you like an ice cream?" Tibbs asked. "Come on, I'll buy you a large one."

Bibi went to Mr. Smith's school and she told Tibbs that

there was going to be a painting competition and that she was planning to enter a large picture.

"What are you going to draw?"

"A cat," said Bibi.

"Do you like cats?"

"I like all animals." She licked her ice cream.

"When you've finished your painting, bring it along to show me," said Tibbs, and he set off for home.

Miss Minnie had now been living in the attic for a week and it was working out very well, everything considered. All it meant was that he now had two cats instead of one.

Minnie slept in the box. And she usually slept all day. At night she went out on the roof through the kitchen window. She prowled across the rooftops and through the back gardens, chatting to the many cats in the neighborhood, and then came back home to her box toward morning.

Her most important task was to find news for Tibbs. To begin with it had been Fluff who diligently hunted for information. But Fluff wasn't a real news cat. He usually came back with gossip about cat fights or about a rat in the harbor or about a fish head he'd found somewhere. He seldom bothered with human news.

The biggest source of news was the Scruffy Cat. She knew everything that was going on. This was because she was a stray cat and raided the trash cans of all sections of the community. And she had a very extensive family, too. The Scruffy Cat's children and grandchildren lived all over the town.

Every night Minnie met her on the roof of the Building Society, bringing with her a plastic bag of fish each time.

"Thank you," the Scruffy Cat would say. "My daughter, the Council Cat, is waiting for you at the City Hall. She's

[33]

sitting on one of the stone lions at the front and she's got some news for you." Or, "The butcher's cat has something to tell you. He's in the third garden to the left, near the chestnut tree . . ."

And right away Minnie would climb down the Building Society fire escape, slink across a courtyard and creep through a back gate into an alley. From there she would go to the agreed place where one or other of the cats would be waiting for her.

"We'll have to start meeting somewhere else soon," said the Scruffy Cat. "I've got a feeling that my kittens are going to be born any day now and I'll have to stay with the little brats instead of coming up onto the roof. But it won't matter because the information service will carry on as usual. All the cats are in the know. They all know that your human is waiting for news and they're keeping their ears to the ground. They're listening and looking everywhere. They'll pass on anything that they hear."

"Where are you going to have your kittens?" asked Minnie. "Have you found a suitable place?"

"Not yet," said the Scruffy Cat. "But I'll find something."

"Why don't you come to us? To the attic?"

"Out of the question," snapped the Scruffy Cat. "Foot-loose and fancy-free, that's me. Do stop going on about it."

"My human is very nice," said Minnie.

"I know. He's a good person, if you can ever call a person good. But I don't really like any of them. They're all right when they're children. Sometimes. Do you know Bibi?"

"No."

"She's painting me," said the Scruffy Cat. "She's painting my picture. She thinks I'm beautiful just as I am, big stomach and all. Makes you think, doesn't it? Anyway, I'll let you know where I am when the time comes. Somewhere in the town, somewhere close to a radio."

"Why close to a radio?"

"I always like to have background music when I give birth," the Scruffy Cat said. "Makes it easier somehow. And more cheerful. Remember that when *your* time comes."

Whenever Minnie came home with a new item of news and told Tibbs where it came from he would say, "What an organization! One cat passes it on to the next—it's a sort of cats' press agency."

"I'm not sure I like that word," Minnie said doubtfully. "Cat press. It makes me think of squashed cat."

"Not a cat pressing agency," said Tibbs. "A cats' press agency."

The arrangement had been his salvation. He thought it was wonderful.

Once, when he came in, he found Minnie sitting quietly in a corner of the room, peering at a small hole in the wall, just above the floorboards.

"Miss Minnie! Not another of your bad habits! Waiting by a mouse hole! That's not very ladylike, is it?"

She stood up and rubbed her head against his hand.

"And you mustn't do that either," Tibbs said with a sigh. "Young ladies don't ask to be stroked. I do wish you'd forget these catty habits."

"*Catty* isn't the right word," said Minnie. "It's *cattish.*"

"All right, cattish then. It seems to me that you're getting more and more cattish all the time. It would be much better if you mixed with people more. And not just with cats. You shouldn't go out on the roof so often and you ought to go outside more during the day."

[35]

"Oh, I can't, Mr. Tibbs. I'm frightened of people."

"What rubbish! Why on earth should you be frightened of people?"

She gave him a searching look with her slanting eyes and then looked quickly away.

What a stupid thing to say, he thought. Especially as *I'm* so timid and shy. After all, *I* much prefer the company of cats.

But he decided to be stern, even so.

"And what do you think you're doing now?" he snapped.

Minnie was washing herself. She was licking her wrist and then rubbing the wet wrist behind her ear.

"Well, that beats everything!" Tibbs said.

"I'm only doing this to make it happen faster," Minnie stammered.

"To make what happen faster? Washing yourself?"

"That would be much faster in the shower. No, turning back into a cat, I mean. I keep hoping it will happen. Oh, I really *do* wish that I was a cat again."

Tibbs sank down onto the sofa.

"Listen," he said. "I want you to stop all this nonsense. You never were a cat, you're imagining it, it was a dream."

She said nothing.

"Honestly," Tibbs went on, "it really *is* nonsense."

Minnie yawned and got to her feet.

"I'm going to my box," she said.

Fluff rubbed around her legs and together Minnie and the gray cat went to her box in the storeroom.

Tibbs called after her, "Well, just supposing that you *were* once a cat, exactly whose cat were you, then?"

There was no answer. All he could hear was a gentle purring miaow. A conversation in Cattish. Two cats talking together in the attic.

Chapter 5

The Secretary

One afternoon, when Tibbs was climbing the stairs to his attic, he heard a furious screeching coming from above his head. It sounded just like two cats fighting.

He took the rest of the stairs three steps at a time and ran into his living room.

They had a visitor. But this was no friendly tea party.

The little girl, Bibi, was sitting on the floor, with Minnie opposite her. There was an empty box beside them and they were both holding on to *something*. And they were both screaming at each other.

"What's going on?" cried Tibbs. "What have you got there?"

"Let go!" Bibi shrieked.

"What is it?" Tibbs asked again. "*Miss Minnie!* Will you let go this instant!"

Minnie shot him a glance. She seemed more like a cat than ever. There was a sly, murderous look in her eyes and she wouldn't let go. She closed her hand with its sharp little nails even tighter around *something*.

"Let go, I said!"

She backed away and hissed angrily at him but still she

wouldn't let go. Before he realized what had happened, she had scratched him very painfully on the nose.

And then Tibbs saw what the *something* was: a white mouse. Still unhurt.

Bibi picked up the mouse tenderly and put it in the box. She was crying with fright and indignation.

"It's *my* mouse," she sobbed. "I brought him here to show you and then *she* jumped on him. I'm going home. I'm never coming here again."

"Wait a minute, Bibi," said Tibbs. "Don't go yet. Listen to me, please. This is Miss Minnie. She's—she's—" He thought quickly. "She's my secretary and she really didn't mean any harm. On the contrary, she really loves mice."

Minnie had risen to her feet and was staring at the closed box. It was obvious that she really *did* love mice but not quite in the way that Tibbs meant.

"Isn't that right, Miss Minnie?" Tibbs asked firmly. "You didn't mean that poor mouse any harm, did you?"

Minnie lowered her head. It looked as though she was going to rub her head against him and he stepped quickly aside.

"What else have you got there, Bibi?" Tibbs pointed to a big collection can.

"I'm collecting money," Bibi said. "It's for the present. The present for Mr. Smith's anniversary. And you've got blood on your nose."

Tibbs touched his nose. There was blood on his hand when he took it away.

"It's nothing," he said. "I'll put something in the can, Bibi."

"And I've come to show you my painting too," said Bibi. She unrolled a large sheet of paper and Tibbs and Minnie both said, "It's the Scruffy Cat. Doesn't she look wonderful!"

"It's for the painting competition at school," said Bibi. "I brought it to show you."

"It's beautiful," said Tibbs, and he felt a drop of blood dribble down his nose. "I'm now going to look for some bandages," he said sternly. "I do hope you'll be able to behave yourself while I'm away, Miss Minnie." He put the box with the mouse inside on his desk, gave her a warning look and then backed out of the room.

He kept an ear open as he rummaged in the medicine chest. They might start brawling again at any moment.

I've got a secretary, he thought. That sounds really good, it sounds very distinguished. Even if she *is* a secretary who'll eat white mice if she gets the chance.

He went quickly back into the room with a bandage stuck crookedly on his nose and he found to his amazement that they'd become great friends while he'd been away. The box with the mouse inside was still standing on his desk, out of harm's way.

"May I have a look at the attic?" asked Bibi. "All of it?"

"Of course," said Tibbs. "Have a good look around. I've got another cat—I mean, I've got a cat too. He's called Fluff but he's outside somewhere. Miss Minnie, would you like to show Bibi around? Then I can get on with some work."

As Tibbs sat down at his desk he could hear the two of them whispering in a corner. He was glad that Minnie had found a friend and when Bibi was about to go he said, "Will you come back and see us sometime?"

"Yes," said Bibi.

"Don't forget your collection can. I put something in it."

"Oh, yes," said Bibi.

"And don't forget your painting."

"Oh, yes."

"And don't forget the box with the—hm, well, you know what I mean." He didn't dare say the word "mouse" in his secretary's hearing.

"Oh, yes."

"And I hope you win first prize!" Tibbs called after her.

Underneath, in the rest of the house below the attic, lived Mrs. Damson.

Luckily Tibbs had his own front door and his own staircase so that he didn't need to go through her house whenever he came in or went out.

That afternoon Mrs. Damson said to her husband, "Put that newspaper down a moment. I want to talk to you."

"What about?" asked her husband.

"About our neighbor upstairs."

"Oh, you mean the young man? Tibbs, you mean? What about him?"

"I think he's got someone with him."

"What do you mean? What do you mean, 'got someone with him'?"

"I think he's got a woman living there."

"Well, that's nice for him," said Mr. Damson. And he picked up his newspaper again.

"Yes, but she seems a very *odd* young woman to me," his wife went on.

"Well, it's none of your business," he said.

There was silence for a while. Then she said, "She sits on the roof all the time."

"Who does?"

"That woman. She sits on the roof at night."

"How do you know?" asked Mr. Damson. "Do you sit on the roof at night too?"

"No, but whenever the lady next door looks out of her attic window she sees her sitting there. With a couple of cats."

"You know that I don't hold with gossip," Mr. Damson said grumpily. He continued reading while his wife went to answer a ring at the front door.

It was Bibi with her collection can.

"Would you like to contribute to Mr. Smith's anniversary present?" she asked.

"Of course," said Mrs. Damson. "Come in and sit down for a moment."

Bibi sat down on a chair with the can on her knee, the painting under her arm and the box with the mouse close beside her.

"Tell me, have you been upstairs at all?" Mrs. Damson said casually. "To the attic?"

"Yes," said Bibi. "To see Mr. Tibbs and Miss Minnie."

"Miss Minnie?" Mrs. Damson said sweetly. "Who's that?" She put a coin in the can.

"His secretary."

"Oh, really?"

"She sleeps in a box," said Bibi.

Mr. Damson peered at her over his glasses when he heard this. "In a box?"

"Yes, in a big cardboard box. She just fits in nicely. Curled up. And she always goes out onto the roof through the skylight. And she talks to cats."

"Oh," said Mr. Damson.

"She can talk to any cat she likes," said Bibi, "because she used to be a cat herself."

"Who said so?"

"She said so. And now I really have to go."

"Don't forget your can," said Mrs. Damson. "And here, there's this roll of paper too. And your box."

When Bibi had gone she said, "Now then, what did I tell you? Didn't I say that the young woman upstairs was odd?"

"A little strange, perhaps," said Mr. Damson. "But I still insist that it's nothing to do with us."

"Now listen," she said. "It's *our* attic, when all's said and done. Tibbs rents that attic from us. And I'd like to know exactly what's going on under my own roof."

"What are you going to do?" her husband asked.

"I'm going up there."

"Just like that? What are you going to say?"

"I don't know yet. I'll think of something."

Mrs. Damson put on her fur coat, even though it was a warm spring day and even though she only needed to take two steps outside.

She would have rung the bell but there was no need as Bibi had left the front door open. Mrs. Damson went up the stairs. It was a long steep staircase and she soon felt very hot in her thick fur coat.

"Hello, Mrs. Damson," said Tibbs.

"Hello, Mr. Tibbs. I hope you don't mind me walking in on you like this—"

"Not at all, come in. Won't you take off your coat?"

"No, no. I'm only staying a moment," Mrs. Damson said as she came into the living room.

There was no one there, apart from Tibbs.

"Oh, you *have* arranged it all nicely," Mrs. Damson said, having a good look around. "What a nice little kitchen. And such a lovely view over the rooftops."

"Would you like a cup of tea?"

"No, thank you. I've only popped in for a moment. I just wanted to say that I always read your articles in the paper. Such nice little articles . . . That must be storage space, I suppose. There, behind that partition. Do you mind if I have a look?"

"There's only junk in there," said Tibbs. "Old chairs, old boxes and so on . . ."

But she had slipped past him, chattering happily.

"I think it's all so fascinating!" she said "A quaint old corner of an old attic."

[45]

Tibbs followed helplessly after her. Now she was bending over the big cardboard box. The wooden floor creaked under her weight.

Minnie woke up. She opened an eye. Then she jumped out of the box with a shriek.

Mrs. Damson backed away in fright. Angry cat eyes glared at her. A hand with sharp pink nails moved towards her and there was a sound of hissing.

"I'm so sorry," stammered Mrs. Damson, and she took a couple of steps backwards. She turned and was about to run away when Tibbs said cheerfully, "May I introduce you to my secretary, Miss Minnie? And this is Mrs. Damson, who lives downstairs."

Mrs. Damson turned around nervously. The strange creature was just an ordinary young woman who was standing grinning at her.

"Pleased to meet you," said Mrs. Damson.

"Are you sure you won't sit down?"

"No, no, I really must go. It was so nice of you to show me your home."

She glanced at the bandage on Tibbs's nose and said, "Good-bye for now."

When she had gone, Tibbs gave a deep sigh and said, "This is her attic. I rent it from her."

"How awful!" said Minnie.

"Why awful? All I do is pay the rent. We don't need to have anything else to do with her."

"I didn't mean that," said Minnie. "I meant how awful, there must be at least twenty."

"Twenty? Twenty what?"

"Cats."

"Twenty cats? Where?"

"In that coat," said Minnie with a shudder. "That fur coat. I was asleep in my box when I suddenly woke up and saw twenty dead cats."

"Oh, so that's why you hissed at her. I thought you were going to scratch her. You really must learn to keep yourself under control, Miss Minnie. You can't scratch someone just because she's wearing a coat made from cat fur."

"I don't see why not," said Minnie. "If she comes here again, I really *will* scratch her."

"Don't be ridiculous. She bought that coat in a shop and the cats were already dead by then. This is what comes from not mixing with people. You shouldn't go out onto the roof so much. You should go out into the street more."

"I went into the street last night."

"You must go out into the street in daylight. Go out shopping. Just like other people."

"All right. But I'll wait until it's dark," said Minnie.

"No, the shops will be closed. Go *now*."

"I can't."

"Go out and buy some bread and biscuits," Tibbs went on.

"I'm scared."

"And we've run out of fish. You can stop by the fishseller on the way. He has a stall on the corner of Market Square."

"Oh dear," said Minnie. "I suppose I'll get used to it. Once I've been out into the street."

"Of course you will," said Tibbs. "You'll get used to it in time. Only—"

"What?"

"I'd rather you didn't ask the fishseller to stroke you."

Chapter 6

Out and About

Minnie walked down the street with a shopping basket on her arm. This was the first time that she had been out in daylight since the day she arrived at Tibbs's attic. She only really knew the town from the rooftops at night.

She felt like creeping along and hiding in doorways or behind parked cars. The people and the traffic made her feel very nervous.

"But there's no need for me to creep along," she said to herself. "I'm just out shopping, that's all. Here comes a dog. But I've no need to be afraid—he's only a very small dog. Still, I mustn't hiss at him. And I certainly mustn't sniff the trash cans. I'm out shopping just like everybody else."

Minnie could smell the fishseller's stall long before she reached Market Square and she started to walk more quickly.

When Minnie reached the stall she walked around it in wide circles a couple of times until she suddenly remembered that she could actually *buy* fish now. She had a purse. There was no need for her to beg and she didn't need to steal.

She went up to the fishseller. He smelled delightful and

she stealthily rubbed her head against his sleeve. He didn't notice because he was busy cleaning herring.

She bought some herring and haddock and mackerel, several of each, and when she had paid for them she rubbed her head against the fishseller's sleeve again. He gave her a puzzled look but Minnie had already walked on in the direction of the baker's shop.

She passed Mr. Smith's school. The windows were open, and she could hear children singing and see them sitting inside. Bibi was among them.

A cat came along then and sat on the fence. The School Cat. "Come on, sniff noses," he said.

Minnie leaned forward and felt the cold pink nose of the School Cat against her own. This was the way in which the cats of the town greeted each other—if they weren't quarrelling with each other, that is.

"If you'll give me a piece of fish," said the School Cat, "I'll give you some news for the paper."

Minnie gave him some fish.

"It's wonderful news," said the School Cat. "England's Admiral Nelson has defeated the French Navy. At the Battle of Trafalgar. Make sure it gets into the newspaper."

"Thanks very much," said Minnie.

Two houses further on sat Cross-Eyed Simon, Mr. Smith's Siamese cat.

"Give me a bit of fish," he said, "and I'll tell you something."

When he'd been given a piece of fish, he said, "You mustn't take any notice of the School Cat. He always listens to the history lessons at school. He finds it all very exciting. But he thinks that it's only just happened."

"I know that," said Minnie. "What was it you wanted to tell me?"

"Just that," said Simon.

"You only said it to try and get some fish," said Minnie. "It's just as well I've got a lot with me."

Then she came to the factory. It was a deodorant factory. Perfume sprays were made there and it smelled horribly of violets. Not nearly as nice as the fishseller's stall.

Minnie was about to hurry past when the factory cat came up to her. The Deodorant Cat was a son of the Scruffy Cat. He smelled very strongly of violets.

"I expect you'll give me some news if I let you have a piece of fish," said Minnie.

"How'd you guess?" asked the cat.

"You can have a little bit of mackerel."

"Well, to begin with," said the Deodorant Cat, "the nicest canteen boy in the factory has just been fired. He's over there. His name's William. It's such a shame because he was always so kind to me and stroked me every day."

"Why did he get fired?" asked Minnie.

"He was always late."

"Well, I'm sorry about that," said Minnie, "but it isn't really *news*, is it?"

"Isn't it? Well, I did say that it was just to begin with. Now here's something else. They're planning to expand the factory. I sat in on a secret meeting today. This whole area will become one enormous deodorant factory."

"Now that *is* real news," said Minnie. "Thank you very much indeed."

"But they haven't got planning permission yet!" the cat called after her. "They have to get that from the Council."

Minnie hadn't met many people on her shopping expedition. But she *had* met plenty of cats and she met quite a few more on her way to the baker's.

The baker's wife was standing behind the counter and there were a couple of women in the shop. Minnie waited politely for her turn but while she was standing there, looking around, the baker's cat came mewing into the shop from the apartment upstairs.

Minnie's first thought was that the cat was going to ask her for some fish. Until she heard what the cat was saying.

"Miaow, miaow!" cried the cat. "Tell the woman. Quickly."

Minnie ran up to the counter and said, "Your little boy has got hold of a bottle of aspirin. Upstairs, in your bathroom."

The baker's wife looked at her in fright, dropped some doughnuts onto the counter, and ran out of the shop without saying a word.

Minnie could tell that the two women in the shop were staring at her. She felt very embarrassed and wanted to walk out, but just then the baker's wife came back.

"You were right," she panted. "I got upstairs and there he was—only three years old—with the bottle of aspirin—pouring it out—you can't leave them alone for a minute. Thank you so much for warning me."

Suddenly she stopped and stared at Minnie.

"But how exactly did you know?" she asked. "You can't see into my bathroom from here."

Minnie wanted to say that the cat had told her but the women were staring at her so she stammered, "I—I—I just had a feeling about it."

"Well, thanks very much anyway. Whose turn is it?"

"The young lady can go first," the two women said.

Minnie bought bread and biscuits. And she paid for them.

As soon as she had left the shop, the others started to talk behind her back.

"That's Mr. Tibbs's young lady . . ."

"She's his secretary and she sleeps in a box . . ."

"And she sits on the roof at night . . ."

"A very strange woman . . ."

"Well," said the baker's wife when she had heard everything, "she may be a strange young woman but she's done me a very good turn. And that's the end of it. A small loaf of whole wheat, did you say?"

Meanwhile Tibbs sat and waited.

It was now more than an hour since Minnie had gone out to do some shopping. To get bread and fish. Why was she taking so long?

He sat at his desk, nervously biting his nails. Just as he was wondering whether to go and find her, the telephone rang.

"Hello," said Tibbs.

"Mr. Tibbs, this is Mrs. Damson. From downstairs. I'm phoning from a telephone booth. Your secretary is up a tree. And she can't get down."

"Oh, thank you very much," said Tibbs.

"Don't mention it."

Then he suddenly remembered to ask which tree it was but it was too late. She had hung up.

"Here we go again!" Tibbs sighed as he ran down into the street. "What a nuisance!"

He ran to Market Square first. There were lots of trees there.

When he arrived, he saw her right away. A crowd of people was standing around. It wasn't the same tree as before but a different one, even taller. Bibi was there too because school had just got out.

"She was chased by a dog," said Bibi.

"Yes, yes," Tibbs sighed. He'd guessed as much. "How are we going to get her down again?"

"The fishseller's doing it," said Bibi. "He's up in the tree. He's helping her down."

Watched by a large audience, Minnie was helped down from the branches, first onto the roof of a vegetable truck and then onto the ground.

"Thank you very much indeed," she said to the fishseller, and she sniffed his sleeve for the last time. "Oh, I left my shopping basket somewhere."

Tibbs picked it up. There were bread and biscuits in it and a very small piece of fish.

"We really must do something about it," said Tibbs when they got home once more. "It really can't go on like this, Miss Minnie."

She was sitting in a corner, looking very sorry for herself.

"It was the same dog as before," she said. "He's called Mars."

"It's not just this tree-climbing," said Tibbs. "It's all your other cat characteristics as well. You really must forget about them."

"It was wonderful being rescued by the fishseller," Minnie said dreamily.

Tibbs grew even more cross then, but before he could say anything, she said, "Oh, I heard some really interesting news while I was out." She told him about the extension to the deodorant factory. It calmed him down a little—he now had something to write about again.

Chapter 7

Your Sister Was Here

There was no sign of the Scruffy Cat when Minnie went out onto the roof that night. A different cat was waiting for her. The School Cat.

"She sends her regards," he said. "But she can't come."

"Has she had her kittens yet?"

"About seventeen, I believe," said the School Cat.

"Where are they?"

"Do you know the parking lot behind the garage? It's best to go through the gardens until you reach the hawthorn tree and then climb through the hedge. There are some abandoned trailers in the parking lot. She's living in one of those. For the time being."

"I'll go right away," said Minnie.

"Give me a piece of that fish before you go."

"It's not meant for you, it's for the Scruffy Cat. I'll take some milk with me too."

"I don't need any milk. But if you give me a piece of fish I'll tell you some news. For the paper."

Minnie gave him a very small piece.

"President Lincoln has been shot," said the School Cat. "Make sure it gets in the newspaper right away."

"Thanks," said Minnie. She guessed that he'd been listening to another history lesson at school.

Passing through the dark gardens, she reached the garage where cars were repaired during the day. The garage was closed but the filling station was open; lights were shining and music could be heard from the radio that played all night long.

It looked as though the Scruffy Cat had got her wish. Background music.

The parking lot at the back was dark. And very quiet. There were some cars there and a small row of trailers at the far end.

Any ordinary person would have had great difficulty finding the way there in the dark but Minnie could see perfectly well and easily found the way to Scruffy Cat's home.

It was an old deserted trailer. One of the windows was broken and the curtains were flapping in the wind. The door stood half open. Inside, the Scruffy Cat was lying on an old blanket. Beneath her lay a huddle of kittens.

"Six of them!" the Scruffy Cat said resentfully. "*Six!* Would you believe it? What have I done to deserve this? Come out from under there, you little monsters!" she said to the kittens. "There, you can see them better now. One of them's ginger. He's just like his father, the Garage Cat. And the rest are all tortoiseshell, like me. And now give me something to eat, I'm starving."

Minnie knelt down and looked at the six wriggling kittens.

They had very tiny tails and blind little eyes and very small claws. She could hear the faint sound of the radio in the distance.

"Do you hear that?" said the Scruffy Cat. "Friendly, isn't

it? I've got every comfort here."

"Are you sure it's quite safe?" Minnie asked. "Whose trailer is this?"

"Nobody's. It's been empty for years. No one ever comes here. I don't suppose you happened to see the Garage Cat on your way over, by any chance?"

"No."

"He hasn't *once* come to have a look at his children," said the Scruffy Cat. "Not that I want him to but even

so . . . Give me the fish now. And I see you've brought some milk too. In a bottle. Do you honestly expect me to drink out of a *bottle?*"

"It's all right, I brought a bowl with me too."

While the mother cat noisily lapped the milk, Minnie took a good look around. "I wouldn't feel at ease here," she said. "A parking lot means people. Lots of people during the day."

"We're in a very quiet corner here," said the Scruffy Cat.

"But your children would be much safer in Mr. Tibbs's attic."

The Scruffy Cat made an angry movement, knocking her kittens roughly aside. They began to squeal plaintively.

"Oh, do shut up!" their mother shouted angrily. "All they ever do is guzzle all day long and then yell blue murder at the slightest excuse!"

Then she gave Minnie a nasty look with her fiery yellow eyes. And she hissed: "If you take my children, I'll scratch your eyes out."

"Take them? Naturally I'd want you to come too."

"Thanks for the offer. But I like it here."

"I'll find homes for them later on, when they're bigger."

"No need. They can take care of themselves. They'll be stray cats, just like me. Never live with people. I've always said that people can be divided into two kinds. Those who are monsters . . ."

She paused and took a large bite of boiled fish.

Minnie waited patiently.

"And the other kind?" she asked.

"I've forgotten the other kind," said the Scruffy Cat.

"Chchchchchch . . ." She suddenly began to make a choking sound.

[60]

Minnie slapped her thin shoulders. The Scruffy Cat spat out a fish bone.

"That really would have been the last straw," she said. "Choking on a fish bone. Make sure that doesn't happen again next time you bring me fish. It isn't easy for me, you know, with this wretched kitten kindergarten under my feet all day. But do you know what the best thing is about being here? I'm nice and close to the big gardens." She waved a paw. "All the posh houses are just over there."

"There are dogs there too," said Minnie.

"Sometimes, but they're usually chained up. And the blackbirds in the gardens are just as fat as the women who live in the houses. And they all leave their back doors open in this weather. You can sneak inside and there's always something worth grabbing. It would really be so much better if *you* came and lived here too. Why don't you? There's plenty of room. We could go out hunting together! And I wouldn't be at all surprised if you'd soon become a proper cat again once you'd eaten a nice fat thrush . . . Darn, that reminds me!"

"What's the matter?"

"How stupid of me," said the Scruffy Cat. "I haven't told you my piece of news. All this motherly love made me forget."

"It doesn't matter, tell me now."

"It isn't news for the paper. It's news for *you*. Your aunt has been here. Your Aunt Molly. She wants to speak to you but she's too old to go up on the roof and so she left the message with me."

"What does she want?"

"She asks if you'll go along and see her. She's had a visit from your sister."

Minnie was startled. "My—my sister? But she lives a long way away. Right on the far side of town. What's she doing over here?"

"Don't ask me," said the Scruffy Cat. "I don't know anything about it. And when you come tomorrow make sure that there aren't any bones in the fish."

"Would you mind if my human came to visit you?" asked Minnie. "And Bibi?"

"I don't mind Bibi," the Scruffy Cat said without hesitation. "She painted my picture. Have you seen it?"

"It's lovely," said Minnie.

"But as for that Tibbs, I'm scared that he'll make trouble for me," said the Scruffy Cat. "He's a real troublemaker, that one. Even worse than you. He might take my children away, and find doctors and injections and *homes* and—"

"I'll tell him that he mustn't make any trouble," said Minnie. "See you tomorrow."

On her way home, Minnie called in at Aunt Molly's garden. She hid among the bushes and then, when she miaowed, her old aunt came outside through the cat flap.

"You haven't made much of an effort, have you?" Aunt Molly said disapprovingly. "Still no tail, still no whiskers, and still that ghastly outfit."

"I heard that—" Minnie began.

"Yes, that's right," Aunt Molly interrupted her. "Your sister was here."

Minnie shivered and her voice was a little husky as she asked, "My sister from Queen's Road?"

"Yes, of course your sister from Queen's Road," said Aunt Molly. "She's the only sister you've got, isn't she?"

"She chased me away," said Minnie. "Out of the house

[62]

and out of the garden. She was angry with me. Because I wasn't a cat anymore. She said I could never go back."

"Quite understandable," nodded Aunt Molly. "But she sends her regards. She isn't cross anymore. She feels sorry for you."

"Then I can go back again?" asked Minnie. "Does she want me back?"

"Not as you are now," said Aunt Molly. "You must become a proper cat again. That goes without saying."

"It was a lovely garden, there on Queen's Road," said Minnie. "It was my own garden and my own house, and the woman was kind to us. Does the woman want to have me back?"

"Of course she does, *when* you're normal again," said Aunt Molly. "And shall I tell you something else? Your sister now knows how it all happened—this sickness of yours. It happened to her too."

"*What?*" shouted Minnie. "Has she also—"

"Ssh, not so loud," said Aunt Molly. "No, she hasn't *also*, but she very nearly did. She got some human characteristics. Her whiskers fell out, her tail began to disappear. It was all because you both ate from the garbage can of the Institute. That's what your sister says, anyway."

"So that's where it came from," said Minnie. "It was the building next door to our house on Queen's Road. There was always a garbage can outside. And I *did* find something to eat there once."

"Exactly," said Aunt Molly. "You ate more of it than your sister did. The effect has worn off with her."

"By itself? Did she get better all by herself?"

"No, she says that she found a particular remedy, something that made her normal again. But if you want to find out exactly what it is then you must go and visit her."

"Oh," said Minnie.

"And I'd do it as soon as possible, if I were you," said Aunt Molly. "It's been going on for quite long enough. Well, what are you waiting for?"

"I don't know that I really want to," said Minnie.

"You must be out of your mind!" cried Aunt Molly. "It's your only chance to become a respectable cat again. And you say that you don't know if you really want to?"

"I can't decide," said Minnie.

Aunt Molly turned indignantly away and went back inside. Minnie went home to her roof, where she sat for a while and watched the moon rise above the Building So-ciety. From the gardens below rose the scent of flowers and in the gutter there drifted all kinds of interesting cat smells. It was all very confusing.

The next morning Tibbs gave her a package.

"A present," he said. "Because I've been given more money at work."

"How lovely, thank you very much," said Minnie.

It was a pair of gloves.

"They're for the party."

"Party?"

"There's a party at the Hotel Monopoly this evening. To celebrate Mr. Smith's anniversary. And I would very much like you to come with me, Miss Minnie. There'll be lots of people there."

"Then I'd much rather not come with you," Minnie said.

"It'll be very good for you," said Tibbs. "And for me too. We're both shy and we must both Make an Effort. I think the fishseller's going to be there too."

"Oh," said Minnie.

"I bought those gloves," said Tibbs, "because I thought that if you just happen to scratch someone, it won't hurt them so much."

Chapter 8

Mr. Smith's Party

"I'd really much rather go home," said Minnie. "I don't think I can face it."

They were standing in Market Square outside the Hotel Monopoly. This was where Mr. Smith's party was being held. There were a great many cars parked outside and a great many people were going in.

Even though Minnie was wearing her new gloves, she still felt very shy when she saw all the bustle.

"Don't be scared," said Tibbs. "Look, Bibi's coming outside."

Bibi came skipping up to them, her face beaming with pleasure.

"What have you got there?" Tibbs cried. "A camera!"

"The first prize," said Bibi. "I won first prize in the painting competition."

"And very well deserved too!"

"It's hanging on the wall," said Bibi. "Inside the hotel. All our paintings are on show today. And I helped make the presentation."

"Are you coming back inside with us?" asked Minnie.

Bibi shook her head. "It's just for the grown-ups this

evening," she said. "We've already had *our* party. At school."

She walked away, and Tibbs said, "Come on, Miss Minnie, let's go inside. And please remember, no purring, no hissing, and no rubbing your head against people, not even the fishseller."

"There won't be any dogs, will there?" Minnie asked anxiously.

"No, dogs don't go to parties."

It was crowded inside. Mr. Smith and his wife were sitting on a platform surrounded by bouquets of flowers, and the children's paintings were hanging on the wall behind them. It was an attractive display and the Scruffy Cat was in the place of honor. A sign underneath her picture read *First Prize*.

"Ah, there you are!" cried Mr. Smith. "It's Tibbs! My dear Tibbs, I'm so glad you could come. Come and look at the present that you've all given me. A color television set! Isn't it marvelous?"

Tibbs shook his hand and said, "This is my secretary, Miss Minnie."

"Pleased to meet you," said Mr. Smith. "Haven't I seen you somewhere before? In a tree?"

Other well-wishers came up then and Tibbs and Minnie walked away. People were standing in small groups, talking to each other. There was the fishseller. He waved to Minnie and she went red. And there was the baker's wife, who nodded to her. Minnie began to feel more at ease.

It's going well, thought Tibbs with relief. There's nothing cattish about her this evening.

Mrs. Damson was there too, in her fur coat. She was standing talking to some other ladies, who nudged each other and looked in their direction.

Miss Minnie grew worried again. "Take no notice of them," said Tibbs.

They came to a table on which were plates of delicious things to eat. Little sausages on sticks. And pieces of cheese on sticks.

"Can we help ourselves?" asked Minnie.

"In a little while," said Tibbs.

Then a big man came in. He was wearing glasses and a striped suit.

There was a sudden hush in the room. Everyone greeted him very respectfully.

"Is that the Mayor?" Minnie whispered.

"No," Tibbs whispered back. "He's the owner of the factory. Mr. Elbow. He's extremely important. And he does a lot of good."

"What sort of good?" asked Minnie.

"He gives lots of money to Worthy Causes."

Minnie wanted to ask some more questions but everyone around them called out, "Ssh! Mr. Elbow is going to speak." They all pushed to the front and Minnie and Tibbs became separated in the crush.

Tibbs was left at the back while Minnie was pushed to the front, right up against the little table where Mr. Elbow was standing.

"Mr. Smith," he began. "Ladies and gentlemen . . ."

Everyone was quiet.

"It gives me a great deal of pleasure to see so many of you here this evening," said Mr. Elbow.

He was holding his car keys in his hand as he spoke. He swung them gently to and fro above the table.

Tibbs looked at Minnie and saw to his horror that her

eyes were following the swinging keys back and forth as if she was at a tennis match. She wasn't listening at all; she was simply spellbound by the swinging keys, just like any cat who sees something moving.

She's going to give them a wallop any minute now, Tibbs thought. He gave a very loud cough but she took no notice.

". . . many of us have sat in Mr. Smith's classes," the speaker was saying. "And we all—"

Wham!

Minnie's gloved hand slammed the keys out of his hand. They clattered onto the little table.

Mr. Elbow stopped talking in surprise and looked at Minnie in amazement. Everyone else stared at her angrily. She looked now just like a cornered cat, desperate to escape. Tibbs tried to push his way to the front, but then she suddenly dropped to the floor and disappeared among all the legs in the direction of the buffet. She was gone.

Luckily Mr. Elbow carried on with his speech right away and everyone soon forgot the incident.

Tibbs peered around. He bent down to look under the table—perhaps she had hidden underneath.

The speech ended and Mr. Smith said a few words in reply. Then glasses were handed around on trays and the people ate snacks. Tibbs wandered unhappily among the drinking, chattering guests. Where was she?

Perhaps she had slipped outside without anyone noticing? Miss Minnie was very good at creeping about and walking quietly and slipping away without being seen. Perhaps she was already at home in her box in the attic.

Tibbs sighed. It had all been going so well. She hadn't hissed at anyone and she hadn't scratched. She hadn't even rubbed her head against the fishseller. Instead she had done something else. Something else that was cattish.

Minnie hadn't gone home. Without anyone noticing, she had gone through a door and found herself in another room. A smaller room, a sort of sitting room. There were a table and chairs and, in a corner, a rack of indoor plants. There was a goldfish tank next to it, standing on a small cabinet.

There was no one else in the room and she made straight for the fish tank. Two sad fat goldfish were swimming around with gaping mouths and bulging eyes. They flicked their tails from time to time, quite unconcerned.

Minnie bent over the fish tank.

"I really mustn't do this," she said to herself. "This is a really cattish thing to do. Any minute now I won't be able to stop myself. Get away, Minnie. Turn around!"

But the fish were like magnets. Two golden magnets. She couldn't keep her eyes off them. She couldn't stop her right hand in its elegant glove from moving towards the tank, right above it, and—

There was a sudden sound of voices outside and she pulled her hand away just in time. And she hid behind the plant rack just in time, as the door opened and two people came in.

One was Mr. Smith. The other was Mr. Elbow.

Minnie crouched down, completely hidden by hanging and climbing plants. She kept very quiet.

"I'll only keep you for a moment," said Mr. Smith. "It's so crowded in there and so much more peaceful here. What I wanted to say was that we, the people in this district, would like to start a society. The Association of Animal Friends."

Aha, thought Minnie, behind the plants. More news for Mr. Tibbs. I must listen carefully to this.

"You know that there are many friends of animals in Chillthorn," said Mr. Smith. "Nearly everyone has a cat. The purpose of our association would be to help animals as much as possible. We want to open a sanctuary for stray cats, we would like to have an animal hospital, and we plan to show films about animals. I myself," Mr. Smith went on, "I myself am preparing a lecture about cats. It will be titled 'The Cat through the Ages.'"

Another piece of news, thought Minnie.

"All I wanted to ask," said Mr. Smith, "was whether you

would be willing to become the Chairman of our Association of Animal Friends."

"I see," said Mr. Elbow. "But why are you asking me?"

"You are so well known," said Mr. Smith. "And so much respected in the town. And, of course, you are known to be a friend of animals. I believe that you yourself have a cat?"

"I have a dog," said Mr. Elbow. "Mars."

Minnie began to shake so violently in her corner that the plants began to shake too. *Mars!* That was the dog who had twice chased her up a tree.

"Well, now," said Mr. Elbow. "I would dearly like to oblige, of course, but you know how it is. I'm so terribly busy. I belong to so many organizations and so many committees. And I'm chairman of the Child Welfare Society . . ."

"There wouldn't be much work involved," said Mr. Smith. "You would have hardly anything to do. We would be so honored just to have your name associated with us. Everyone has so much respect for you."

Mr. Elbow wandered up and down the room with his hands behind his back. He gazed at the goldfish for a while and then came up to the plant rack and peered at the plants for a long time.

He's seen me, thought Minnie.

But all he did was pull a dead leaf from a geranium and say, "Very well then."

"Wonderful, wonderful!" cried Mr. Smith. "Thank you very much indeed. We will get in touch with you shortly. And now I must get back to my party."

They went out of the room and Minnie was able to breathe again.

She emerged from her hiding place and saw an enormous

black cat sitting on the windowsill. The hotel cat. The Monopoly Cat.

"This room is out-of-bounds," said the cat. "I'm not allowed in. Because of the goldfish. Have you seen them?"

"I nearly caught one," said Minnie. "I must get back to that room where all the people are, but I'm scared."

"Your human's looking for you," said the Monopoly Cat. "He's out at the front, on the terrace. If you climb through the window you can go around outside. Then you won't need to see all the people."

With one jump, Minnie was outside.

"Good-bye," she said and walked around to the front where Tibbs was pacing up and down.

"Miss Minnie—" he began severely.

"I've some more news for you," she said.

She told him what she had overheard and Tibbs nodded gratefully.

When they were back home in the attic he said, "I still think that you ought to do something about—about all these *cattish* qualities of yours. And your *cattish* behavior."

"What *can* I do about it?"

"I think you ought to go and see a doctor."

"I'll do no such thing," said Minnie. "Doctors give injections."

"I don't mean an ordinary doctor."

"What then? A vet?"

"No, I mean a talk-doctor. He is a special doctor you go to see when you have *problems*. You go and talk to him."

"I don't have any problems," said Minnie.

"No, but *I* do," said Tibbs.

"Then *you* go and see a talk-doctor."

"It's because of *you* that I've got the problems, Miss Minnie. Because of your strange habits. It was all going so well at the party to begin with. You were behaving beautifully until you suddenly slapped Mr. Elbow's keys with your p—with your hand. Secretaries don't do that sort of thing."

Chapter 9

The Talk-Doctor

A nd so it was that Minnie found herself the next day in a doctor's office.

"First of all, may I ask your name?" the doctor said.

"Miss Minnie."

"Is Minnie your surname? Or your first name?"

"It's what people call me," said Minnie.

"And what is your surname then?"

She was silent for some time, watching a fly buzzing on the window. At last she said, "I don't think I have one."

"Well, what is your father called?" the doctor asked.

"Ginger next door."

"Well, then, that's your name too." The doctor wrote on the card: Miss M. Ginger-Next-Door.

"Now, perhaps you could tell me what's troubling you."

"Troubling me?" said Minnie. "Nothing's troubling me at all."

"But you wanted to talk to me. There must have been a good reason for you to come here."

"Yes. My human says that I'm too cattish."

"Too what?"

"Too cattish. And he says that I'm getting more and more cattish all the time."

"I expect he means that you're very similar to a cat."

"That's right," said Minnie.

"Well, then," said the doctor. "Let's begin at the beginning. Tell me something about your parents. What did your father do?"

"He strayed," said Minnie. "I never knew him. I can't tell you anything about him."

"And your mother?"

"My mother was a tabby."

"I beg your pardon?" The doctor looked at her over his glasses.

"She was a tabby. But she's no longer alive. She was run over."

"Passed over," mumbled the doctor, and he wrote it down: Mother Passed Over.

"Not passed over, *run* over," said Minnie.

"How dreadful," said the doctor.

"Yes, she was dazzled by the headlights. It was a semi. It all happened a long time ago."

"Well, carry on. Have you any brothers or sisters?"

"There were five of us."

"And you were the eldest?"

"We were all the same age."

"Quintuplets? How very unusual."

"Not really," said Minnie. "It happens all the time. Three of us were given away when we were six weeks old. I was left with my sister. The woman thought we were the nicest."

She smiled at the memory, and, in the silence that followed, the doctor could hear her purring quite distinctly. It was a very peaceful sound. He was very fond of cats and had one himself. She lived upstairs in his apartment.

[77]

"The woman?" he asked. "Was that your mother?"

"No," said Minnie. "The woman was the woman. She said that I had the most beautiful tail."

"Aha," said the doctor. "And when did you lose it?"

"Lose what?"

"The tail."

She gazed at him thoughtfully, looking so like a cat that he began to wonder if she still had the tail. Perhaps it was still there under her skirt, all curled up.

"I once ate something from a garbage can," said Minnie. "The Institute garbage can. And that's when it happened. But I've still got plenty of cattish qualities. I purr and I hiss. And I climb trees whenever a dog comes along."

"And does this cause problems? Is it a nuisance?"

"Not to me," said Minnie. "But my human doesn't care for it much."

"Who is your human?"

"Mr. Tibbs from the newspaper. I'm his secretary. It's working out very well but I still feel like a cat."

"And does that cause you any problems?" the doctor asked.

"It can be a bit complicated," said Minnie. "And it's sometimes very confusing being two different creatures at the same time. Half cat and half person."

"Ah," said the doctor. "It can also be very confusing being a complete person, believe me."

"Really?"

"Yes, indeed."

Minnie had never thought of that. She found it an interesting idea. "All the same, I'd much rather be one or the other," she said.

"And which would you prefer?"

"That's just it. I don't really know. I just don't know. Sometimes I think that I'd really like to be a cat again, and creep through the lilacs with my tail held high so that the blossoms fall on my fur, and sing on the rooftops with the other cats, and go hunting in the garden when the young starlings are learning to fly. But on the other hand, it's fun being a human too."

"You'll just have to wait and see what happens," said the doctor.

"I was wondering," said Minnie, "if you could give me some medicine. Or something. So that—"

"So that what? So that you can be a cat again?"

"No," said Minnie. "I don't think so."

"You'll have to make up your mind first," said the doctor.

"And then come back and see me. I haven't got any medicines or pills for you but talking can always be of help."

There was a scratching at the door. It was the doctor's cat.

"My cat wants to come in," said the doctor. "But she knows it's not allowed when I have a patient."

Minnie listened to the mewing outside the door.

"She wants you to go upstairs," she said. "Your wife has started to fry the chicken . . ."

"How do you know that we're having chicken for lunch?" the doctor asked.

" . . . and she's burned her thumb on the pan and she wants you to go up right away," said Minnie. "I'll be going now, doctor, but I'll come back when I know what I want to do."

The doctor ran upstairs to his apartment. His wife was standing angrily by the stove. She had a big blister on her thumb.

"How did you know what had happened?" she asked.

"A very nice cat told me," the doctor said and went to fetch some ointment.

Minnie was on her way home when she heard the dreadful news about the Scruffy Cat. It was Cross-Eyed Simon who told her.

"How terrible!" said Minnie. "Her leg, did you say? Has she broken it? Was it a car? And where is she now? Is anyone with her children?"

"Don't ask so many questions all at once," said Cross-Eyed Simon. "It may not be as bad as it sounds. I heard it from the Garage Cat and he always exaggerates so. She was hit."

"Hit?"

"Someone hit her with a bottle. But she managed to drag herself home to the trailer and her kittens."

"I must go to her at once," said Minnie. "I'll take her some food, and some milk."

She found the Scruffy Cat in the trailer with her kittens, even more grumpy and bad-tempered than usual.

"What happened?" asked Minnie as she knelt by the blanket. "Is it bad? Is your leg broken? Is there any blood?"

"They've crippled me!" said the stray cat. "With a full bottle of wine. Oh, do help yourself! Don't mind me! I suppose I should feel honored to be bashed on the leg by a bottle of burgundy."

"Let me see if anything's broken," said Minnie.

"Get your filthy hands off me!" screeched the Scruffy Cat.

"I only want to feel."

"But there's nothing *to* feel. Keep your hands to yourself."

"But if you've broken your leg something must be done about it."

"It'll wear off. I'm all in one piece."

"But I should take you somewhere. To our attic."

"I don't want to go anywhere. I'd rather put up with it. I'm fine here."

Minnie sighed and gave the Scruffy Cat the milk and some meat.

"That came just in time," said the cat. "What a thirst I had! I always drink by the tap in the parking lot. There's a puddle of water underneath it. But it's a long way away, and I can't walk as easily as I used to . . ."

When she had drunk her fill she said, "It was all my own stupid fault."

"Tell me what happened."

"I was walking through the posh gardens," said the Scruffy Cat. "I came to that big white mansion with all those roses. I usually don't go in that garden because they've got a dog. But this time the dog was shut in the garage. He was barking his head off but I didn't take any notice because he couldn't get at me. The windows were open and there were some really wonderful smells inside. And I was so hungry. With six yowling brats like these, you're hungry all the time, believe me. Anyway, I looked inside. And there was no one in the room. There was a big table with a bunch of roses. I couldn't care less about roses but I could smell salmon. And, well, you know how it is. You grab your chances where you can."

"You went inside?"

"Of course I went inside. I jumped on the table and landed right on top of the salmon. And then I saw there was lots of other stuff too. Lobster and chicken and cold beef. Whipped cream and shrimps and all kinds of dishes with all kinds of sauces. And lots of other goodies too . . . yummm!" The Scruffy Cat started to drool all over her kittens.

"And then what happened?"

"Keep quiet and I'll tell you. I started to feel quite giddy. Because of all that food. I just didn't know where to begin, you see. I must have been out of my mind. If only I'd eaten the salmon, then at least I'd have had *something*. But all those smells went right to my head, and I just stood there. And to think I let an opportunity like that slip through my paws! Without so much as a taste! Meeeuw!"

"Come on, what happened then?"

"Well, what do you think? All at once I saw them standing there."

"Who?"

"The people. The man and the woman. I didn't hear them come in. It sounds stupid, I know, but there you are— I was in such a whirl. I dived off the table and made for the window but *she* was standing there with an umbrella and she lashed out at me. So I went back but *he* was standing on the other side. He'd grabbed a bottle of wine from the table. And it really hurt! Miaow!" The Scruffy Cat howled at the memory.

"How did you get out?"

"I've no idea. All I know is that I *did* get out somehow. I think I skidded between her legs and she walloped me with the umbrella but I can't be sure. I shot into the garden. I didn't notice anything was wrong at first until I tried to jump over the hedge. Then I knew for sure. I couldn't jump

[83]

anymore. I couldn't even climb."

"How did you get over?" asked Minnie.

"The dog. They let the dog out of the garage. I could hear him coming, he'd almost reached me, and there was no hole in the hedge. Nowhere. I really thought I was done for. Crippled, and with a dog like that coming for me—well, I didn't stand a chance. But I gave him a good scratch on the nose and he backed off a bit. And when the brute came at me again I thought about my kittens and I got over the hedge. How, I don't know, but I got over somehow."

"And how's the walking now?" asked Minnie.

"Terrible. I can only just drag myself along. But I'll get over it. It's all part of the game. It's the price you pay for being a stray. But at least I managed to give that dog a clout that he won't forget in a hurry."

"What was the dog's name?" Minnie asked.

"Mars."

"What?"

"Oh, do you know him?"

"I know him all right," said Minnie. "So it was his human who hit you?"

"Yes, of course. I told you, didn't I? His name's Elbow. He's the owner of the deodorant factory. Where my son the Deodorant Cat lives."

"He's also the chairman of a society," said Minnie. "The Association of Animal Friends."

"Well, well," said the Scruffy Cat sadly. "There you are, you see. It doesn't surprise me in the least. People—they're all rubbish."

"How dreadful!" Bibi said when she heard the story. "What an awful man. Poor Scruffy Cat."

"You must go and pay her a visit," said Minnie. "You know where she is."

"Yes, I've already been there once. In the old trailer. Would she mind if I took a photograph of her kittens?"

Bibi carried her camera everywhere and took photographs all over the place. The pictures were usually a bit crooked but very clear.

Bibi and Minnie had become good friends. They were sitting together on a bench in the park.

"Has Tibbs put it in the paper?" Bibi asked. "Mr. Elbow and Scruffy Cat, I mean."

"No," said Minnie. "He says he's not allowed to write about cats."

"But it's not just about cats! It's about the—the chairman of—what was it again?"

"The Association of Animal Friends."

"Well, that should go straight into the paper, shouldn't it? A man like that crippling a poor mother cat."

"Yes, it should," said Minnie. "But he won't do it."

She looked past Bibi at a branch of a nearby elm tree. Bibi followed her gaze. A bird was sitting on the branch, singing. She looked at Minnie and gasped. There was something very nasty in that gaze, just like that time with the mouse . . .

"*Minnie!*" Bibi screamed.

Minnie jumped.

"I didn't do anything," she said. But she looked very guilty, all the same.

"You must *never* even think of it," said Bibi. "A bird is just as precious as a cat."

"When I lived on Queen's Road . . ." Minnie said dreamily.

[85]

"When you lived where?"

"On Queen's Road. As a cat. I caught birds then. Behind the house, in the lilac tree beside the terrace, that's where I caught the most. And they were so . . ."

"I won't listen to another word of this!" Bibi shouted, and she ran away with her camera.

Chapter 10

Cats Can't Give Evidence

"I don't understand it," Minnie said for the umpteenth time. "It *must* go in the paper. Scruffy Cat Crippled by Chairman of Animal Friends."

"No," said Tibbs. "My boss says that cats aren't news."

"A poor old mother cat hit by a bottle," said Minnie. "She's lucky to have got away with her life."

"I can quite see that someone might get very angry if they suddenly found a stray cat in the middle of their salmon," Tibbs said. "I can see how they might just grab the first bottle that came to hand to knock the cat off the table."

"Really?" said Minnie. She gave Tibbs such a nasty look that he took a step backwards, remembering her sharp nails.

"Anyway, it's not suitable for the paper," he said. "And that's the end of it."

Whenever Minnie was angry, she always went into her box to sulk. She was just about to do this now when Fluff came in through the kitchen window with a plaintive miaow.

"What's he saying?" Tibbs asked.

"The fishseller!" cried Minnie.

"Rrow . . . wheeuw . . . rrow," Fluff went on. He told her what seemed to be a really enthralling story in Cattish and then disappeared onto the roof again.

"What's happened to the fishseller?" Tibbs asked.

"He's in the hospital!"

"Really? It sounded as though Fluff was telling you a really amusing story."

"The fishseller has been run over," said Minnie. "His stall and everything. By a car. All the cats in the neighborhood are there now because the fish are lying all over the street."

"I'll go there right away," said Tibbs. "I can write a report about it." And he picked up his notebook.

"I'm coming too," said Minnie. "Over the roof, it's quicker."

She was just about to climb out of the kitchen window when Tibbs pulled her back. "No, Miss Minnie. I don't want my secretary to be seen slobbering over an upset fish stall like any old stray cat."

Minnie gave him a very haughty look.

"And anyway," Tibbs said, "there'll be a lot of people there and you won't like that."

"Very well, I'll stay here," said Minnie. "I'll hear all about it on the roof, anyway."

There were indeed a great many people in Market Square. A crowd, in fact. The police were there too. There was broken glass on the street and the fishseller's stall was in ruins; there were bits and pieces lying everywhere, and the last cat was just running away with the last fillet.

Mr. Smith was watching too.

"They've taken the fishseller away," he said. "To the hospital. He's got a broken rib."

"How did it happen?" Tibbs asked.

"It was a car! But the funny thing is that no one knows *which* car. It drove away. Scandalous!"

"Didn't anyone see it happen? In broad daylight?"

"No," said Mr. Smith. "It happened at lunch time, and everyone was indoors, eating. They just heard a bang and when they came outside the car had already gone around the corner."

"And what about the fishseller himself?"

"He doesn't know, either. One moment he was cleaning

herring and the next he was lying on the street with the stall on top of him. The police have questioned everyone in the area but no one saw the car. It must have been a stranger, someone from out of town."

Tibbs looked around. A cat was sitting eating on the corner of the square. I bet the cat saw who did it, he thought. And I bet Minnie already knows.

He was right.

"We've known who did it for a long time now," Minnie said when Tibbs came upstairs again. "It's the talk of the rooftops. It was Mr. Elbow's car. And he was driving. He was the one who did it."

Tibbs looked at her in disbelief. "Come on, now," he said. "Why would a man like that drive away after an accident? He would have reported it right away."

"The cats saw everything," said Minnie. "As you know, there are always cats around the fishseller's stall. Cross-Eyed Simon was there and the School Cat and Cassock the Church Cat. I'm glad that you know about it now, Mr. Tibbs. It can go in the newspaper."

Tibbs sat down and started to bite his nails.

"That's right, isn't it?" Minnie asked. "It *will* go in the newspaper?"

"No," said Tibbs. "I shall certainly write a story about the accident. But I can't say that Mr. Elbow did it. There's no proof."

"No proof? But three cats —"

"Yes, cats. But what has that got to do with it? There isn't any evidence."

"There were three witnesses."

"Cats can't give evidence."

"Oh, no?"

"No. I can't write in the paper that according to the eye-witness reports of several cats, the fishseller was knocked down by our most eminent citizen, Mr. Elbow. I just can't do it. Surely you can see that?"

But Minnie couldn't see. She went silently to her box.

That night on the roof, Cross-Eyed Simon said, "Someone's waiting for you at the City Hall."

"Who?"

"The Deodorant Cat. He's got some news."

Minnie went there right away. It was three o'clock in the morning and very quiet in the square. In front of the City Hall, two stone lions sat on their haunches in the moonlight, each with a stone shield between its knees.

Minnie waited. From the shadow of the left-hand lion there came a mixture of strange scents. She could smell cat and perfume. And then the Deodorant Cat appeared.

"Sniff noses first," he said.

Minnie stuck out her nose.

"Sorry about the smell of apple blossom," said the cat. "It's our latest fragrance. I've got something to tell you but you mustn't let anyone know that you heard it from me. I don't want my name in the paper. Will you promise me that?"

"I promise," said Minnie.

"Well now, do you remember me telling you about William? William the canteen boy who was fired?"

"Oh, yes," said Minnie. "Well?"

"He's back again. He's been given his job back."

"Well, that's very nice for him," said Minnie. "Is that all?

The newspaper won't be interested in *that*."

"Hang on a minute," said the Deodorant Cat. "I haven't finished yet. Listen to this. I was sitting on the ledge this afternoon. There's a ledge on the wall outside and if I sit there in the ivy I can hear everything that happens in the owner's office. Did you know that Elbow is the owner of the factory?"

"Of course I know," Minnie shouted. "He crippled your mother."

"Exactly," said the cat. "And that's why I hate him. Not that I have all that much to do with my mother. She has an awfully common sort of smell. I'm used to more delicate aromas now. But that's neither here nor there. As I was saying, I was sitting on the ledge. And I saw William in the office with Elbow and I thought I'd better have a listen, just in case."

"Go on," said Minnie.

"I heard Elbow say: 'Well, that's all settled then, William. You can come back. Get back to work right away.' And William said: 'Yes, sir, very good, sir, thank you very much, sir.'"

"And that was all?" asked Minnie.

"I thought so at first," said the cat. "I thought that was all and so I decided to have a little doze. Well, the sun was shining and you know how it is, especially if you're sitting on a ledge . . . "

"Yes, yes," said Minnie. "Go on."

"Well, suddenly I heard Elbow saying very quietly by the door, 'And remember, if anyone asks if you saw anything today in Market Square, you saw nothing at all. Understand? Absolutely *nothing*.' And William said, 'Yes, sir.' And he went out of the office. And that was that."

"Aha!" said Minnie. "I understand now. William saw the accident!"

"That's what I think too," said the cat.

"And so we now know that a human saw the accident too," Minnie said to Tibbs. "A proper witness. Not just a cat witness."

"I'll go and see William right away," said Tibbs. "Perhaps he'll admit that he saw something. If I come straight out with it."

He went.

While Tibbs was away, Minnie had a conversation on the roof with the cat from the hotel. The Monopoly Cat.

"Now listen," said Minnie. "I hear that Elbow sometimes comes to your hotel for a meal. Is that true?"

"Yes," said the Monopoly Cat. "He comes for dinner once a week, with his wife. On Fridays. He'll be there this evening again."

"Would you mind sitting under his table?" Minnie asked. "And listening to what he says?"

"You must be joking!" said the Monopoly Cat. "He gave me a kick under the table once."

"Look, it's like this," said Minnie. "We really want to know what he says. But none of us dares to go to his house and listen. He's got that dog, you see. Mars. So if you could get as close to his table as possible . . ."

"I'll see what I can do," promised the Monopoly Cat.

Much later, Tibbs came home, very tired and dejected.

"I've been to see William," he said. "But he says that he didn't see anything. He claims that he was nowhere near Market Square when it happened. I think he's lying. He obviously doesn't dare say anything. I've also been to see the fishseller in the hospital."

"How is he?" asked Minnie. "Does he still smell nice?"

"He smells of hospital," said Tibbs.

"That's a pity."

"I asked him if the car could have been Mr. Elbow's. But he got very angry and said it was a stupid idea. Elbow is his best customer and he'd never do anything like that. Then," Tibbs went on, "I also went to the police. And I asked them if it could have been Mr. Elbow's car."

"And what did they say?" asked Minnie.

"They laughed out loud. They thought it was a really stupid question."

Chapter 11

The Garage Cat and the Monopoly Cat

"Hasn't your human written anything about Elbow in the paper yet?" the Scruffy Cat asked.

"No," said Minnie. "He hasn't got any evidence, he says."

"What a coward!" cried the Scruffy Cat. "How yellow can you get! I just don't understand humans at all. They're about as much use as dogs." She was so angry that she forgot all about her children. One of the kittens had crawled as far as the trailer door. When the mother cat saw it, she shouted, "Hey, where do you think *you're* going? Going for a stroll, are you? Come here, you miserable brat!" She grabbed her child by the scruff of the neck and dragged it back to its nest on the blanket. "They're starting to be a nuisance," she said. "The little horrors."

The kittens now had their eyes open. They were very lively and played with each other's tails. And with their mother's thin and skimpy tail too.

"How's your leg coming along?" Minnie asked.

"It's getting better. I still walk with a limp. I probably always will now. Whenever I go to have a drink from the puddle under the tap the journey seems to take forever."

"And you have to leave your children alone all that time?" Minnie asked anxiously. "Is that really wise?"

"No one ever comes here," said the Scruffy Cat. "Except you and Bibi. She brings me something every day too. And today she took photographs of all these monsters. Imagine taking pictures of these ugly little beasts! Makes you think . . . Oh yes, before I forget. Their father, the Garage Cat, asks if you'd go over to see him. He's got something to tell you. I can't think what but it's probably got something to do with the fishseller's accident."

Minnie said good-bye and walked to the garage. The Garage Cat greeted her cheerfully.

"I don't know if it's of any use or not," he said. "But I thought it wouldn't do any harm to let you know."

"Tell me anyway," said Minnie.

"Elbow was here. He had a big dent on the side of his car. And one of the headlights was broken."

"Ah," said Minnie.

"He's got two cars," said the Garage Cat. "It was the

biggest, the blue Volvo. You know that we've got a filling station here as well as a garage. Anyway, he told my human, the mechanic, that he'd driven it into his own garden hedge and he wanted the car to be fixed today. And my human said that it would be difficult."

"And then?" asked Minnie.

"Then Elbow gave him some money. I couldn't see how much it was. But it must have been an awful lot because my human looked really pleased. And then Elbow said, 'If anyone asks you about the dent in my car, I'd rather you didn't say anything at all.'"

"*Aha!*" Minnie said again. "Many thanks."

As she went she called out, "You've got lovely children."

"Who has?" asked the Garage Cat.

"You."

"Me? Who says so?"

"The Scruffy Cat."

"She talks too much," the Garage Cat said bitterly.

The Monopoly Cat was a shiny black tom with a white chest. He was also very fat, thanks to his comfortable life in the hotel dining room. At meal times he wandered slowly among the tables, looking at everyone with a pathetic pleading gaze that seemed to say, "Can't you see that I'm starving?" Most of the guests gave him something and so he grew fatter and fatter. He waddled as he walked.

It was half past seven on Friday evening and the dining room was fairly full. Waiters were bustling about, knives were clattering on plates, and people were eating and talking. There was a smell of roast beef and potatoes.

In a corner of the room, a little apart from the others, sat Mr. Elbow and his wife.

The Monopoly Cat moved nervously towards them. He had promised Minnie that he would try and listen to what they said but he wasn't too sure about it as this was the man who had once given him a kick under the table. He sat down a safe distance away. He could tell from their faces and their gestures that they were quarreling but they were quarreling in whispers and so he couldn't hear.

I'm definitely not going to sit under the table, the cat thought. I don't want another kick. But nothing much can happen if I go and sit by her chair.

So he sat close by and listened.

". . . remarkably stupid of you," he heard Mrs. Elbow say. "You should have reported it at once."

"Don't start all that again," said Mr. Elbow. "Stop going on about it."

"And you *still* haven't reported it," she went on. "You still can, you know."

He shook his head firmly and helped himself to some more meat.

The Monopoly Cat took a step closer.

"Scram, you pesky cat!" Mr. Elbow hissed. But the cat stayed where he was, looking hungry and innocent.

"Don't talk such nonsense," Mr. Elbow went on. "It's far too late now. Of course you're right, I *should* have reported it right away. But what's done is done. I can't do anything about it now."

"But what if it all comes out—"

"It won't. No one saw what happened, apart from a stupid canteen boy I'd just fired. But I gave him his job back right away."

"And the garage where you took the car?"

"The mechanic will keep his mouth shut. He's a good

buddy of mine. Through thick and thin."

"I think you should go and report it," Mrs. Elbow persisted.

"Will you please shut up about it! Do you think I'm mad or something? I've had enough trouble as it is getting the people of this town just where I want them. I've given money hand over fist to one Good Cause after another, just to make people like me, to get *in* with everyone. I've joined societies, I'm chairman of goodness knows what, I sit on committees—all to win the trust of these people. And it's worked too!"

The Monopoly Cat took another careful step forward.

"Get away, you!" Mr. Elbow hissed. "That cat's a real nuisance."

The cat waddled quickly away, made a rapid circuit of the dining room, and came back to his old position again. He heard Elbow say, "Just think what would happen if it got into the newspaper. There would go my good name! I'd never get elected to the Town Council. And I could forget all about the extension to the factory. Everyone would turn against me. So let's forget all about it, shall we? What would you like to eat now?"

"Ice cream," said Mrs. Elbow.

"And if I ever meet that wretched cat one dark night I'll have his guts for garters," her husband said, staring threateningly at the fat black tom cat.

The Monopoly Cat had heard enough. He wandered outside and then struggled onto the roof with great difficulty in order to report to Minnie.

"But it's still only a cat who heard what he said," Tibbs complained. "Again it's not real evidence. How can I write a report without a single shred of proof? And the only two people who could help me won't say anything. William and the garage man. They still maintain that they don't know anything."

"But do you believe the cats now?" Minnie asked.

"Yes," said Tibbs. "I believe you."

"I wish that I could give that Elbow a really good scratching," said Minnie.

"I wish you could too," said Tibbs.

He was beginning to feel very disheartened. He now knew for certain that the cats were speaking the truth but he didn't dare write about it without any evidence. And as well as being disheartened, he was beginning to feel angry. Angry and indignant. And his anger was making him less timid. He was able to go straight up to people now and ask them anything he liked.

But when he happened to remark casually to Mr. Smith that he'd heard someone say that Mr. Elbow had caused the accident to the fishseller, the teacher said angrily, "Whatever gave you *that* idea? Who's spreading stories like that? Mr. Elbow would never do such a thing. Apart from anything else, he's a very careful driver and, anyway, he'd report an accident like that immediately. He would never drive off. No, Tibbs," Mr. Smith went on, "you're talking absolute nonsense, my boy. What you've said is gossip, nothing but idle gossip."

Chapter 12

The Scruffy Cat's Children

One morning, Mrs. Damson, who lived in the house underneath Tibb's attic, said to her husband, "I used to have a little green teapot somewhere. I wonder what could have happened to it?"

"No idea," said Mr. Damson. Then, a little later, he said, "Didn't we keep that teapot in the trailer? Our old trailer?"

"Yes, of course. You're right. Then it will have gone for scrap with the trailer. That old trailer was sold for scrap, wasn't it?"

"Now that you mention it," Mr. Damson said thoughtfully, "I think it's still in that parking lot. Do you know the one I mean?"

"All these years?"

"Yes, a very long time."

"I'm going to have a look," said Mrs. Damson. "The teapot may still be there. It was such a nice little pot. And there may be other things that we can make use of."

And so it was that Mrs. Damson arrived at the parking lot at the very moment that the Scruffy Cat had gone out for a drink. She had gone to the puddle of water just as she did every day, dragging her lame leg behind her. She always

left her kittens alone but nothing terrible had ever happened to them; they were never disturbed because no one
ever came there.

But this time Mrs. Damson pushed the door open and
went inside.

The first thing she saw was the litter of kittens on their
blanket.

"Oh no!" she cried, making a face. "Not in *my* trailer! A
bunch of kittens, and such dirty little cats too. And they're
on *my* blanket!"

It was a very old blanket, torn and dirty. But this didn't make any difference to Mrs. Damson. She picked up an old cushion cover and stuffed the little cats inside it.

Then she found the green teapot, looked around the trailer again, and said, "There we are, then."

She went away with the teapot in one hand and the bag of kittens in the other.

The Scruffy Cat saw her leaving the trailer but she was a long way away. And she couldn't run. She hobbled back to her home as quickly as she could. A shrill and pitiful cry echoed around the parking lot but no one heard it because the filling-station radio was playing so loudly. And Mrs. Damson wouldn't have taken any notice even if she *had* heard it. She was standing by the gas pump, staring doubtfully at the heavy bag of kittens in her hand.

"What on earth am I going to do with them?" she asked herself. "I can't possibly take them home with me. What am I going to do with six dirty young cats?"

Then she saw that a car was being refuelled. A big blue car. It was Mr. Elbow's car.

Mrs. Damson went up to it. She bent down by the driver's window and said, "Oh, good day, Mr. Elbow."

"Good day, Mrs. Damson."

"I've got a litter of kittens here. I found them in my old trailer. They're in an old cushion cover. May I give them to you?"

"To me?" asked Mr. Elbow. "What on earth would I want with kittens?"

"Well," said Mrs. Damson. "I read somewhere that you're the chairman of the Association of Animal Friends. Isn't that so?"

"Yes, that's so," said Mr. Elbow.

"Well then, the Association is supposed—I mean, it *does* find homes for animals, doesn't it? That's what I read anyway."

"Yes, but I don't really have much time at the moment," Mr. Elbow began.

"And if homes can't be found," Mrs. Damson said, "I'm sure you can take them somewhere to be painlessly put to sleep. Will you see to it then? I'll just put them in the back."

She put the bag of kittens on the back seat of the car, gave him a friendly nod, and walked away.

Mr. Elbow was left with a bag of young cats in his car.

"That woman seems to think that I'm a mobile animal sanctuary," he said angrily. "What *am* I going to do with them?"

He drove away.

The poor Scruffy Cat stayed in the trailer at first, mewing and howling. When she went outside again, Mrs. Damson had gone. But the Garage Cat came running up.

"Your children have been taken away," he said. "In a bag. In Elbow's car. He's driven away with them."

The Scruffy Cat sat down and cried.

She knew that her kittens were lost forever. She knew that there was little point in looking for them because they were probably already dead. And anyway, she had difficulty walking now. She was practically helpless.

"I'll pass on the news," said the Garage Cat. "To the Cats' Press Agency. I don't know if it'll do any good."

The Scruffy Cat couldn't say anything. She just whimpered quietly to herself.

"Now then, stay calm!" said the Garage Cat. "It's awful for you, I know."

He walked away. The Scruffy Cat called after him, "They're your children too, you know."

The Garage Cat turned around. "We have only *your* word for that!" he snarled.

The Cats' Press Agency always worked very swiftly. But no message had ever been passed as quickly as this one. Ten minutes later Minnie had already heard the news from Fluff.

"And where did Elbow go in his car?" she asked at once.

"His car is parked outside the post office."

"And are the kittens still inside?"

"No," Fluff said sadly. "They're no longer there. Simon looked through the window. There's nothing in the car at all."

"Where can they be then?" cried Minnie. "What has he done with them?"

"No one knows," said Fluff. "The Garage Cat saw him driving away and Cassock saw him passing the church. Then a couple of other cats saw the car outside the post office a little later on. But no one saw what he did with the kittens in between."

"Perhaps he's drowned them somewhere," cried Minnie. "Oh, how dreadful for the poor Scruffy Cat. She was always complaining about her kittens but she was so proud of them really. Every cat must look and ask and listen. I'll look too."

She went down into the street and set off in the direction of the post office. The cats she met on her way could tell her no more than she already knew. Not a single cat had seen what had happened to the cushion cover. They had only seen the car being driven along and then, later on, seen it parked, empty.

Minnie had no idea where to look and she wandered aimlessly along back alleys until at last the Baker's Cat came running up to her.

"They've been found!" the cat cried. "The School Cat heard them mewing!"

"Where?"

"In a trash can by the post office. Come quickly, we can't reach them."

Minnie was there within the minute.

All six kittens were still alive. They were still in the

cushion cover and had been stuffed, cover and all, into a big gray trash can. The little creatures were mewing and trembling when Minnie lifted them out, but they were still alive.

A short distance away stood the garbage truck that the Council used to collect the trash. If Minnie had arrived just a few moments later, the Scruffy Cat's children would have been taken away. They would have been smothered . . .

Minnie put the six kittens carefully back into the cushion cover so that she could carry them to safety. And she stroked the School Cat, who had found them.

"That was very clever of you," she said. "Thank you very much. It was just in time."

"And I've got some news for you too," said the School Cat.

"Tell me."

"The Japanese have attacked Pearl Harbor."

Minnie didn't take the kittens back to the trailer. She took them to the attic instead and put them in her own box for the time being.

"What are you doing?" Fluff asked. "Are you planning to keep them here?"

"Of course," said Minnie. "And the Scruffy Cat is coming here too. I'm going to fetch her right away."

"I'm not sure if I approve of all this," Fluff said. But Minnie had already disappeared through the kitchen window.

The Scruffy Cat knew nothing of what had happened. She was walking around and around the trailer. Every now and then she went inside, as if she hoped that her kittens might still be lying there. She mewed helplessly without stopping. However grimy and bedraggled the Scruffy Cat might be, she was usually never pathetic. But she was now. Now she was nothing more than a pitiful stray cat, wretched and miserable.

Until Minnie suddenly appeared on the trailer steps.

"They've been found," she said. "All six of them. They're up at our place. In the attic."

The Scruffy Cat showed no sign of pleasure. All she did was sit up a little straighter.

"Bring them here at once," she snapped.

[108]

"No," said Minnie. "It isn't safe here. You've seen that for yourself now. I've come to fetch you."

"Who? Me?"

"Yes."

"I won't *be* fetched," the Scruffy Cat said with icy contempt. "I won't be fetched by anybody."

"It's only for the time being," said Minnie. "In a couple of weeks we'll find homes for all your children. But until then you must come with me."

"It's out of the question," said the Scruffy Cat.

"Your children need you. They need to be fed."

"Bring them here then and I'll feed them."

There was little point in arguing further. No one could make the Scruffy Cat do anything against her will. She would fight tooth and nail.

But Minnie could be just as obstinate. "If you want them back, you'll have to come and fetch them," she said. "You know where we live."

The Scruffy Cat shouted something after her. The worst swear word that she knew: "*Human!*"

Minnie made a soft bed for the little cats in the corner of the attic. Tibbs wasn't at home; he was wandering around the town, looking for evidence.

"I don't like this," Fluff complained. "I really don't like this at all. Six strange screaming kittens in my attic. Oh well, have it your own way then. Go ahead."

"It's just for the time being," said Minnie.

"Just so long as that mother of theirs doesn't turn up," said Fluff. "That really *would* be the last straw!"

Minnie said nothing. She stood at the kitchen window and looked out across the rooftops.

After an hour the Scruffy Cat came. With her lame leg

she could only climb up to the roof very slowly and with great difficulty. With a mighty effort she dragged herself into the gutter and allowed Minnie to lift her through the window.

She said nothing at all. Minnie said nothing either. She put the Scruffy Cat with her children, who mewed and squirmed with delight and immediately began to drink.

"I don't believe it," said Fluff. "The mother too. And now I really know that I don't like it!"

His tail was fluffed up, his ears were flat against his head, and he was making a bloodcurdling growling sound.

"Control yourself, Fluff," said Minnie. "And keep away from that corner."

As long as the Scruffy Cat stayed with the kittens, everything went well. But the minute she walked away from them, into the kitchen in search of the litter box, then it all began . . .

And it was at that moment that Tibbs came in to find a furious fight in progress. A screeching ball of fur was rolling over and over on the floor and tufts of hair were flying through the air.

"What in heaven's name is going on here?" Tibbs shouted. "Don't tell me we've got another cat?"

"We've got seven more cats," Minnie said as she tried to separate the two fighters.

She told him what had happened.

"You mean to tell me Elbow put live cats into a trash can?" Tibbs asked.

"That's right," said Minnie.

It was then that Tibbs became really angry at last.

Chapter 13

Tibbs Is Writing!

"Eight cats in the house!" Tibbs muttered. "Nine, if I count Minnie. What a ruckus!"

It was indeed a ruckus! The kittens didn't keep still for a minute. They crawled everywhere. They climbed on chairs, they clawed the sofa and the curtains, they sat on Tibb's papers and played with his pen. But he didn't really mind. He even felt rather honored that the Scruffy Cat had come to live with him. He knew that the old stray had always refused point-blank to live with people and yet she had even come and sat on his lap and allowed him to scratch her behind the ears.

"You can live with us for the rest of your life," Tibbs said.

"You must be joking!" the Scruffy Cat cried, and she jumped off his lap. "As soon as those little creeps are big enough, I'm going to be a stray again."

Tibbs didn't understand what she was saying, of course. He was just glad that there was no more fighting. The two big cats spat at each other every now and then and sometimes they sat growling at each other for half an hour at a time, but they kept their distance.

At last Tibbs said, "And now everyone must keep very quiet. I'm going to start writing."

He sat down at his desk with a grim expression on his face.

Minnie asked nervously, "Are you going to write an article?"

"Yes," said Tibbs.

"Oh," said Minnie. "Are you going to write *the* article? About Elbow?"

"Yes," said Tibbs. "And I don't care anymore if I've got any evidence or not. I couldn't care less if there aren't any witnesses."

He began to tap away on his typewriter. Every now and then he stopped to pull a kitten out of his hair. Every now and then he stopped to push a kitten off his papers. He typed busily on.

The Scruffy Cat and Fluff forgot that they were enemies. They sat watching him, silently and respectfully, and the news passed from cat to cat across the roofs of the town: "Tibbs is writing! Tibbs is writing at last! Have you heard? It's going to be in the newspaper. Yes, that's right, Tibbs is writing!"

When Tibbs had finished his article, he went to hand it in. He met the Newspaper Cat when he got to the office. The cat looked at him with respect and admiration for the very first time.

And when he had delivered his article and was walking home across Market Square, he noticed that there seemed to be a lot more cats about than usual. They came up to him, they twined themselves lovingly around his ankles, and they called out, "Well done! At last!"

He didn't understand them. But he knew what they were saying.

Mr. Elbow was sitting in the office of the editor of the *Chillthorn Courier*.

He had spread the morning's paper on the desk and was pointing at an article.

"And what is the meaning of *this*?" he demanded. He was white with rage and his voice was shaking.

Now it was the editor's turn to bite his nails nervously.

"I'm afraid I've no idea," he said. "I've only just read it myself. I can't imagine how it came to be in the paper—"

"I had nothing at all to do with this!" Elbow shouted. "It's all lies! And it's in *your* paper!"

The Newspaper Cat was sitting on the windowsill, his ears pricked and his eyes wide with surprise.

"I'm most terribly sorry," sighed the editor. "The young

man who wrote this is usually so reliable. He writes out-standing stories, he never reports gossip, it's always the truth and—"

"Surely you're not trying to tell me that *this* is the truth?" Mr. Elbow screeched.

"No, no, oh no, of course not—"

How feeble can you get, thought the Newspaper Cat.

"—all I wanted to say was that I usually never need to check his articles beforehand. They're always so accurate. So this one appeared in the paper quite without my knowledge."

"I demand," said Elbow, banging his fist on the desk, "I *demand* that this young man write another article immedi-ately to set the record straight."

"A brilliant suggestion," the editor said with relief. "I'll see to it at once."

The Newspaper Cat had heard enough. He jumped down from the windowsill and hurried to Minnie's roof.

"Listen . . ." said the cat.

Minnie listened.

"Thank you," she said.

And she went inside to tell Tibbs.

"Well," said Tibbs. "At least I now know what to expect."

The telephone rang. It was Tibbs's boss.

"I've got to go the newspaper office," Tibbs said to Minnie a little later. "He wants to talk to me right away."

Nine pairs of cats' eyes watched as he went down the stairs.

"My request is really very reasonable, Tibbs," said the ed-itor. "You've made a terrible blunder. You've written something offensive about an eminent and respected citizen. Offensive and, above all, *untrue*. Where did you get such a crazy idea? Mr. Elbow knocking down the fishseller indeed!"

"It's the truth," said Tibbs.

"What evidence do you have? Where are your witnesses? Who saw it happen?"

"A couple of people know about it," said Tibbs.

"Really? And who are they? And why haven't they said anything?"

"Because they're frightened of Mr. Elbow. He's got them under his thumb. They don't dare say anything."

"Well," sighed the editor. "It seems highly improbable to me. But, as I've said, you now have a chance to put things right. All you need to do is write a favorable article about Mr. Elbow. Naturally you must say that it was all a stupid mistake. And that you apologize. And he would also like you to write something pleasant about the deodorant factory. How wonderful it is to work there. And how many delightful fragrances go into the sprays they make. And how terrible it would be if there weren't any deodorants at all. Everyone would smell to high heaven . . . well, you know what I mean. And how essential it is for the factory to be enlarged. You will do it today, Tibbs. At once. Is that understood?"

"No," said Tibbs.

There was silence for a moment. The Newspaper Cat was back in his place on the windowsill and gave Tibbs an encouraging wink.

"No? What do you mean—*no*? You mean you won't do it?"

"That's exactly what I mean," said Tibbs.

"This is getting serious," said the editor. "You've been in

top form recently. And now you're about to lose your job because of your obstinacy. Please be sensible about this, Tibbs."

Tibbs looked the Newspaper Cat straight in the eyes.

"I'm sorry," he said. "But I can't do it."

"It's a great pity," the editor sighed. "Then I have nothing more to say. You will have to go, Tibbs."

And Tibbs went.

When he was outside again, Tibbs met Mr. Smith.

"What on earth have you done now, Tibbs?" he asked. "I've just been reading the paper and what did I read there? Gossip! Lies! Mr. Elbow is the chairman of our Association of Animal Friends. Do you really think that *he* would bury kittens in a rubbish bin? And knock down the fishseller without reporting it? And just drive on? Where did you get it from, Tibbs? How did you ever get such a stupid idea into your head? Really! And I was just on the point of asking you to come to my lecture on 'The Cat through the Ages.' I was going to ask you to write a report about it. But I'm not sure now if you're the right person for the job."

"I couldn't do it anyway," said Tibbs. "I'm not with the newspaper anymore."

And he walked miserably home.

"And now I really *have* been fired, Miss Minnie," he said. "I kept my job because of the cats and now I've lost it because of the cats. But I don't regret a thing."

He sat down on the sofa and all the cats gathered anxiously around him. Even the little ones sensed that this was a serious moment and played only half-heartedly with his shoelaces.

"Whatever happens, we mustn't give up," said Minnie.

"Something is going to happen tonight. As soon as it gets dark all the cats in the district are going to meet on our roof."

That evening Tibbs stayed at home with the kittens, who were too young for the meeting. He could hear the cats outside.

He had no idea how many cats were there but it must have been at least one hundred, judging by the noise. They screeched and they screamed. And every now and then they sang the Miaow-Miaow Song.

At about eleven o'clock there came a ring at the door.

It was Mrs. Damson. She came wheezing upstairs in her fur coat and snapped, "Mr. Tibbs, I've been talking it over with my husband and we feel that it really has gone quite far enough."

"What do you mean?" asked Tibbs.

"This used to be a respectable house before you came to live here! Now it's been turned into a hotbed of cats. Listen to them! You can hear for yourself."

The cats on the roof burst out singing once again.

"I can't stand anymore of it," Mrs. Damson went on. "And what's *this* I see? Six *more* young cats! I do believe that they're the same little monsters that I found in my trailer. Six kittens plus two big cats and that strange young woman who's more cat than human—that comes to nine altogether! Plus another hundred on the roof, that makes one hundred and nine."

"Plus twenty dead cats," said Tibbs. "That makes one hundred and twenty-nine altogether."

"What do you mean?"

"I mean your coat. There are at least twenty cats in that."

Mrs. Damson now became really angry. "That is the height of impertinence!" she shouted. "My mink coat! Are you trying to tell me that it's made from cat fur? Are you trying to insult me, like you did that nice Mr. Elbow in the newspaper? Yes, I read all about it. It's a scandal. And that's why my husband and I have agreed that you must get out. Out of my attic. With your entire cattery. You can stay until the end of the month. After that I will rent the attic to someone else. Good night to you!"

I shouldn't have said those things about her fur coat,

Tibbs thought when she had gone. Not that it would have made much difference. She would have kicked me out anyway. But it wasn't very polite of me. And now I'm going to bed.

Tibbs went to bed. He was so tired that he didn't hear the cats' chorus outside and he didn't feel the kittens scrambling over his face. He didn't hear Fluff come home. Or the Scruffy Cat yelling at her children to come to her. And he didn't notice Minnie going into her box.

When he woke up it was eight o'clock in the morning. Something awful had happened, he thought. What was it? Oh yes, I've lost my job. *And* I've lost my home. What shall I do now? Where can I go with nine cats, and how will I earn enough to feed such a large family? He went to talk to Minnie but she had gone.

She was sitting in the park with Bibi.

"The cats of Chillthorn have a plan," she was saying. "And we would like your help, Bibi."

"Of course," said Bibi. "How?"

"I'll tell you," said Minnie. "Now listen very carefully."

Chapter 14

A Plague of Cats

Mr. Elbow was walking down the street. He had parked his big blue car, now completely free of dents, and was on his way to a store to buy a pair of shoes.

As he walked he became suddenly aware that there seemed to be an enormous number of cats in Chillthorn. He could hardly take one step without finding a cat at his feet. Sometimes *between* his feet. Twice he stumbled over one.

We ought to get rid of the lot, he thought. It's a plague of cats, that's what it is. I'll bring Mars with me next time.

After a while he noticed that the cats were following him. To begin with there was just one cat walking behind him but when he looked around a little later there were eight.

And when he reached the shop there were more than ten. They all followed him inside.

"Scat!" Mr. Elbow shouted angrily. He chased them out of the shop but they all came in again with the next customer.

They clustered around him while he was trying on shoes and sitting there helplessly in his stockinged feet.

"Are these your cats, sir?" the shop assistant asked.

"Certainly not!" Mr. Elbow shouted. "They've been following me."

"Shall I chase them away?"

"Yes, please."

The cats were chased out of the shop but when the door opened for two new customers, they all trooped in again and crowded around Mr. Elbow's legs.

He longed to give them a kick. He longed to throw a boot at them but there were far too many customers in the shop. And everybody knew who he was. Everyone knew that he was chairman of the Association of Animal Friends. And so he didn't dare kick any of the cats.

At least, not when anyone could see him. I'll just bide my time, he thought grimly. My chance will come soon enough.

And his chance *did* come, a little later. The crowd of cats was following him down the street. He didn't dare do anything while people were looking but when he came to the school, he noticed that the street was empty. He took a quick look around, saw no one coming, and gave the Baker's Cat a hefty kick.

The cats scattered in all directions.

"That'll teach 'em," Mr. Elbow said contentedly. But when he returned to his car, opened the door, and saw eight cats sitting inside, he grew really angry again. He was just about to drag them out when he heard a voice behind him say, "Well, look at that! How sweet!"

He turned and saw Mr. Smith beaming at him.

"All those cats in your car," he said. "You really *are* a true friend of animals!"

"Well, naturally," Mr. Elbow said with a strained smile.

"Are you coming to my lecture tomorrow?" asked Mr.

Smith. "I'm sure you'll find it particularly interesting. 'The Cat through the Ages.' With color slides. You *will* be there, I take it?"

"Of course," said Mr. Elbow.

The cats trooped meekly out of the car. Mr. Elbow drove to his factory. He had an important meeting in his office with the Mayor. To talk about the extension to the factory. But he was late, thanks to the cats. When he went into his office, the Mayor was already there.

Mr. Elbow apologized, offered him a cigar, and began to talk about the extension to the factory.

"Some people don't like the idea of an extension," said the Mayor. "They're worried that there might be too many smells in town."

"Oh, but they'll be very pleasant smells," said Mr. Elbow. "Our newest fragrance is Apple Blossom. Perhaps you'd like to sample it?"

When he turned around to pick up the scent spray, he saw three cats slipping out of the open window.

He opened his mouth to swear at them but stopped himself just in time.

"Just smell how nice this is," he said.

The Mayor sniffed.

"Apple Blossom," said Mr. Elbow. He had a sniff too. But what he smelled was anything *but* apple blossom. The whole room stank of cats.

The Mayor felt like saying, "It's cats' pee." But he had been very well brought up and so instead he said politely, "Mmmm, that smells interesting!"

That afternoon Mr. Elbow took his dog in the car with him, just in case he was followed yet again by a crowd of cats.

And yes, there they were. They were waiting in the parking lot. Some were close by, others a little farther away. The place was swarming with cats.

Mr. Elbow opened the car door and said, "Come on, Mars. Look, Mars! Cats, cats! Get 'em!"

But to his amazement Mars stayed in the car, whining softly. He wouldn't go outside.

"What's wrong with you? Don't tell me you're scared of cats?"

But Mars wouldn't move. He growled angrily but he didn't dare go outside.

He had seen the Scruffy Cat. She was standing close by and although she was lame and not very quick on her feet, she was the bravest of them all. She looked so vicious and so menacing, and she had such a nasty expression on her dirty face . . .

Mars could still feel the scratching that she had given him in his own garden. And there were all those other cats too. There were too many of them, he wouldn't stand a chance. So he stayed inside.

"Call yourself a dog!" Mr. Elbow said scornfully. He looked around. A great many cats and very few people. And no one was watching.

He picked up the dog leash and lashed out with it a couple of times. Cassock the Church Cat was hit and flew shrieking into the church. The others scattered like a swarm of flies.

And then, just like flies, they came back. The Scruffy Cat was at their head. And Mr. Elbow kept the leash by him as he drove away again.

That evening they came into his garden.

Until now Mars had kept any cat away. None had dared go into the garden, except when he was locked in the garage. It was on just such an occasion that the Scruffy Cat had injured her leg.

And now, all at once, there were cats in the garden.

Mars leaped excitedly up and down at the window but he didn't dare go outside.

"I don't understand what's wrong with that dog," Mr. Elbow said angrily to his wife. "He's scared of cats. Have you ever heard of such a thing? A German shepherd who's scared of cats?"

"I do believe they're digging up our roses," his wife said. "Chase them away! Here, take this bottle. You got that filthy stray cat with it last time."

Mr. Elbow ran outside with the bottle.

The cats were busily scratching up his finest and most expensive rose bushes, his pride and joy.

They looked at him in triumph as he came outside.

"Filthy animals! There's no one around to see me now! You're in my private garden. And I'm going to—"

He lashed out on all sides but all he did was trample over his own roses and get scratched very painfully by a thorn. The cats disappeared from view among the trees and bushes.

"You'd better think twice before coming back!" Mr. Elbow shouted at the bushes.

Then he went inside. A moment later his wife said, "They're back again."

"Where?"

"In the roses. All our roses will be ruined."

"I've had enough of this," her husband said grimly. "This has gone too far. Luckily there's no one around to stop me now. Fetch me my hunting rifle."

She fetched it for him.

He stood on the terrace with the gun in his hand. The late evening sun was shining through the branches of the trees onto the flower bed where at least ten cats were busy digging up the roses, their eyes shining with delight.

"I've got you now, you scum!" Mr. Elbow said softly.

He took aim . . .

Simon the Siamese was the nearest of the cats. He squinted at Mr. Elbow but he didn't move.

Seven of the cats slipped nervously away but three stayed where they were. The Mayor's Cat, the Scruffy Cat and Cross-Eyed Simon.

They dashed away in the nick of time, just before the shot rang out. The Scruffy Cat was the last to disappear. She hobbled across the lawn and vanished in the shadows before Mr. Elbow had time to take aim once more.

He turned to go inside again, and then he saw the little

girl. A little girl in his garden. He could see that she was laughing. Laughing at him.

"Who are you? What are you doing here?" Mr. Elbow shouted.

She was laughing so loudly that she couldn't answer.

Mr. Elbow was beside himself with rage now. He seized the child by the arm and shook her hard.

"And now get out of my garden, you little minx!"

It seemed at first as though Bibi was going to cry, but as soon as she was out of the gate she began to laugh again.

She waited in the road by the gate for a moment. Then Minnie came out of the garden through a gap in the hedge. And she was followed by the Scruffy Cat and all the others, one by one.

For the rest of the evening the roses were left in peace.

Chapter 15

"The Cat through the Ages"

"It's the lecture tonight," said Minnie. "Mr. Smith's lecture. In the Hotel Monopoly."

"I know," said Tibbs. "But there's no need for me to go."

"He's going to show pictures," said Minnie. "Of different kinds of cats. In color."

"I'm sure he is," said Tibbs. "But I'm still not going. I don't have any articles to write anymore. I'm no longer working for the newspaper. And I have plenty of cats at home, thank you very much."

"I expect everyone will be there," said Minnie.

"I'm sure they will," said Tibbs. "And that's why I'd rather not go. Mr. Elbow is bound to be there because he's chairman of the Association. And I don't ever want to see him again."

"Well, *I'm* going," said Minnie.

He looked at her in surprise. Was this the same Minnie who had been so shy and so scared of going to places where there were lots of people?

"And I'd be really pleased if you'd come with me," she said.

He could tell from her voice that something special was

about to happen. But he couldn't think *what* and so, after some hesitation, he said, "Oh, all right, then."

There was a notice outside the hotel that read:

Association of Animal Friends
Tonight: *The Cat through the Ages*
An illustrated lecture by Mr. W. Smith

Tibbs and Minnie were the last to arrive. The room was crowded because Mr. Smith was very popular and he was also an entertaining speaker. And the people of Chillthorn were all very fond of cats.

Mr. Elbow was sitting near the front because he would soon have to say a few words of welcome.

The lecture hadn't yet begun, so people were talking among themselves. As Tibbs and Minnie found somewhere to sit they could hear people talking about them.

Two old ladies in the row behind were whispering quietly to each other.

"That's the young man from the newspaper, isn't it? With his secretary?"

"But he's left the paper, hasn't he?"

"Really?"

"Oh, yes. He wrote that scandalous article about Mr. Elbow."

"Oh, so it was *him*, was it?"

"Yes. His name was underneath. He said that our dear Mr. Elbow had knocked the fishseller down with his car."

"That's right, and he also said that Mr. Elbow had put those live cats in a garbage can. It's disgraceful to write that sort of thing without a single shred of evidence."

Tibbs could hear everything they said. He began to feel more and more miserable and wished that he'd stayed at

home. Minnie was sitting next to him with a very secretive
look on her face. She seemed very calm and looked as
though she couldn't care less what people thought.

Bibi was sitting nearby, with her mother.

Then Mr. Elbow stood up to say a few words. He was
greeted with enthusiastic applause.

As the people clapped, they peered furtively at Tibbs. It
was as if they were saying: You wrote an article full of ugly
rumors and we don't believe a word of it. We have faith in
our own Elbow.

Mr. Elbow smiled and bowed. His speech was very short
and then he introduced Mr. Smith.

It was a very interesting lecture. Mr. Smith spoke about
the cats of the ancient Egyptians. Then he spoke about the

cat in the Middle Ages, and he showed slides as he went along. The lights in the hall were put out and whenever he tapped on the floor with a stick, a new cat was shown on the screen.

"There will now be an intermission of fifteen minutes," Mr. Smith said after he had been speaking for an hour. "Refreshments will be available at the buffet. But before we pause, I would just like to show you one picture of a very unusual cat from the Renaissance period."

He tapped with a stick. This was the signal for the boy who was operating the projector to show the last cat before the intermission.

And a cat did indeed appear on the screen. But it was not a Renaissance cat. It was the Baker's Cat receiving a hefty kick in Market Square. And he was receiving the kick from Mr. Elbow, who could be seen very clearly in the picture. It's true it wasn't a very good photograph and that the picture was at an angle, but there was no possible doubt whatsoever.

Tibbs sat up straight in his seat. He looked at Minnie. She smiled back at him.

"That's my cat!" shouted the baker in the second row.

Mr. Smith tapped his stick crossly and called out, "That's not the correct slide."

There was a sound of muttering in the hall. Then another slide came up. This one showed Mr. Elbow busily hitting Cassock the Church Cat with a dog leash. And you could see quite clearly that he was enjoying himself.

"That's our cat!" shouted the pastor.

By now the next slide was already on view. There was Mr. Elbow standing on the terrace in his own garden with a gun in his hand. He was aiming at three cats.

"That's my Simon," Mr. Smith cried indignantly.

"Our cat," whispered the Mayor's wife.

The Scruffy Cat was also in the picture but nobody seemed concerned about her, apart from Tibbs, who looked at Minnie in dismay. She smiled at him again. And suddenly he understood the cats' plan. He realized that Bibi had taken the photographs in the street and in Elbow's garden with her new camera. Only Bibi could have taken such crooked photographs.

There was loud mumbling and whispering in the hall now.

Everyone was looking at Mr. Elbow. It was quite dark in the room but he could be seen standing up and walking to the front.

"It's not true!" he shouted. "It wasn't me!"

Then came the next slide. It was even more crooked than the others but it was very clear, just the same. Mr. Elbow was holding a little girl by the arm and shaking her. The little girl was Bibi.

"It's a lie!" Mr. Elbow shouted. "I can explain. It's nothing but a clever fake!"

But everyone was talking so loudly that no one heard what he said.

He walked to the back of the hall where the projector stood.

The boy who was showing the slides was William, the canteen boy.

"Stop this at once!" Mr. Elbow shouted.

"That was the last one," said William.

"It's you!" Elbow said angrily. "You! Where did you get those slides?"

"I just showed all the slides I was given," said William.

"That was what I was supposed to do."

"Where did the last ones come from?"

"I really don't know," said William.

There was now a great commotion in the hall and Mr. Smith tried to calm everyone down. "Ladies and gentlemen, this is all the result of a dreadful misunderstanding," he said. "I suggest that we all go and have a quiet cup of coffee, after which I shall resume my lecture."

"You're fired!" Mr. Elbow hissed at William.

He went back to the others. The lights had now been turned on and people were talking in groups and wandering across to the buffet. They fell silent when Mr. Elbow came up to them.

He tried to explain everything. But there was nothing to explain. The slides had been clear enough. Mr. Elbow made a helpless gesture and walked out of the room.

When he had gone, the conversation flared up again.

"I just can't believe it," said the Mayor's wife. "The chairman of the Association of Animal Friends! And he shoots cats! He shot at *my* cat!"

"He shook *my* child," said Bibi's mother. "That's much worse. And he's the chairman of the Child Welfare Society too!"

Bibi sat very quietly in her chair, looking as though all this had nothing at all to do with her.

"Why didn't you tell me anything about this?" her mother asked. "Why didn't you tell me what Mr. Elbow did?"

But Bibi didn't say anything. She looked at Tibbs over her glass of cola and whispered, "Good, isn't it?"

"Great!" he said.

"Minnie took the photo of me," she said. "She was up a tree."

Tibbs looked around for Minnie. He had lost sight of her in the crowd. As he walked around the room he heard snatches of conversation.

The two old ladies were talking again.

"It's quite possible that it was true, after all."

"What?"

"That article in the paper. You know, the one that said that Elbow had put kittens in a garbage can."

"Well, of course it was. A man like that is capable of anything. And that business with the fishseller's stall is true, too, of course."

A little way off Mr. Smith was talking to William.

"How could it have happened, William?" Mr. Smith

asked. "Those slides at the end. You weren't supposed to show those. Where did they come from?"

"Miss Minnie gave them to me," said William. "She asked if I would show them before the intermission. I don't know why she wanted me to show them but she was very kind. And she asked me so very nicely."

"I see," said Mr. Smith. "Well, well . . ."

"And now I've lost my job," William went on. "But at least I can say it now."

"Say what?"

"I was there," said William.

"Where?"

"When Mr. Elbow knocked over the fishseller's stall with his car."

"But my dear boy!" cried Mr. Smith. "Why didn't you say so before?"

Someone else came up then. The mechanic from the garage. "I'll tell all I know too," he said. "There was a lot of damage to Mr. Elbow's car."

"You shouldn't tell *me* all this," said Mr. Smith. "You must tell the police. It just so happens that there's a policeman here this evening."

He went up to Tibbs, who was still wandering around on his own.

"Tibbs," said Mr. Smith, "I fear that I've done you a grave injustice. I do apologize. You were right from the very beginning. And now you should write a report of what happened here this evening."

"I'm no longer with the newspaper," said Tibbs.

Minnie was also walking alone among the chattering groups of people. Every now and then she could hear what they were saying:

"Tibbs was right all along . . . he was telling the truth."

"Do you really think so?"

"Oh, definitely!"

And she was satisfied. This was, after all, what the cats had hoped to achieve with their plan.

She was just about to return to her place when she saw something black sitting behind a glass door. It mewed.

Minnie pushed the door open and went into the hotel foyer.

The black shape was the Monopoly Cat.

"I've been calling out to you for ages," he complained. "I didn't dare go in because of the crowd. Did it all go according to plan?"

"It all went beautifully," said Minnie. "Thanks to all the cats."

"Good," said the Monopoly Cat. "But I was calling to

you because there's someone waiting for you outside in the street."

"Who is it?" asked Minnie.

"Your sister. Outside the revolving door, in the shadow of the lime tree. If you come now."

Minnie went hot and cold at the same time. Just as she had in Aunt Molly's garden . . .

"I can't," she said. "I must get back. There's a lecture."

"Come now," said the Monopoly Cat. "What's that lecture to you? How can you think about 'The Cat through the Ages' when there's a cat of today waiting outside to see you?"

"I'm still not going," said Minnie.

"Why not? Surely you're not frightened of your own sister?"

"No—I mean, yes—" Minnie stammered. "Tell her that I can't see her."

When Tibbs came back to his place, Minnie was already sitting there, in the chair next to his.

Mr. Smith's lecture went on, and no more strange things happened.

Chapter 16

The Newspaper Cat

The next morning there was a lot of coming and going on the rooftops.

All the cats were up there. The news had been passed from one cat to the next the night before.

"This is the best news since women got the vote," said the School Cat.

They were all sitting on the roof of the Building Society. Minnie had never seen so many cats in one place before, certainly not in broad daylight. She had brought a bag of meat with her, which she shared with all the others. Cassock was so wild with excitement that she began to screech at the top of her voice in a way that was somewhat out of keeping with a church cat.

"Let's have a party!" she screamed.

"Yes, let's have a party," said the Scruffy Cat. She was proud that she had managed to climb to the highest roof despite her bad leg.

"But there's not very much to celebrate," said Minnie. "My human is still without a job and he's got to find somewhere else to live in a few days' time."

"Just wait a while," said Cross-Eyed Simon. "Anything

might happen today. There's been a change of heart. The people don't like Elbow any more. My human is very angry."

"Yes, mine is too," said the Mayor's Cat.

"The whole town's talking about it," said the Monopoly Cat. "Not just us but the people too."

Meanwhile Tibbs was sitting in his attic, alone except for the six kittens. His big cats were on the roof. So was Minnie.

He had hardly seen anything of her since the lecture and there were all sorts of things he wanted to ask.

He wandered about, feeling a little lost. And then there was a ring at the door.

It was Mr. Damson, who lived downstairs. He came nervously into the room and refused to sit down.

"I've just come," he said, "because I've heard that my wife has terminated your lease. She wants you to leave the attic. She terminated the lease without my knowledge. She shouldn't have done it. I don't agree with her at all."

"Won't you sit down?" Tibbs asked.

Mr. Damson sat down on the edge of a chair.

"She's always been a little impetuous," he said. "She was cross because there were so many cats on the roof. But I told her that it wasn't your fault. It's the area. There are so many cats living around here now."

Tibbs nodded.

"And we don't mind at all that you have cats of your own," Mr. Damson went on. "Well, *she* does but I don't."

"Thank you," said Tibbs.

"And of course she *was* very angry about that article in the paper," said Mr. Damson. "But we know now that you were perfectly right. It was all true. I've just heard that

Elbow knocked the fishseller down. And the police have found a couple of witnesses."

"Oh," said Tibbs. "That's good. I can't offer you a cigarette because I don't smoke but would you like a peppermint?"

"Yes, please," said Mr. Damson. "I believe that you also have a—er—secretary—somewhere." He looked around vaguely.

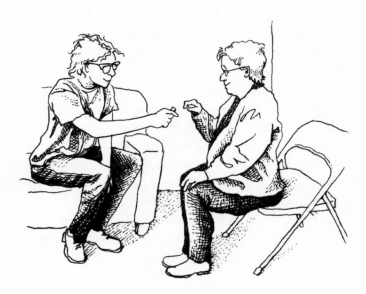

"Yes," said Tibbs, "but she isn't here at the moment. She's out on the roof."

"And what lovely kittens you have," said Mr. Damson. "I'd really like to have one of them."

"Yes, of course," said Tibbs. "When they're bigger."

"Oh, no, I've just remembered that I can't. My wife

doesn't like cats. So I can forget about that idea. But I just want to say one thing, Tibbs. You're welcome to continue living here for as long as you like. And that's the end of it."

"That's wonderful," Tibbs said.

He wanted to tell Minnie right away but she wasn't there. And the minute Mr. Damson went downstairs, the telephone rang.

It was Tibbs's boss.

Could Tibbs come over and see him at once?

Half an hour later, he was sitting in the familiar chair facing the editor's desk. The Newspaper Cat was there too, winking at him.

"It seems you were right all along, Tibbs," said the editor. "Everything you wrote was true."

"Of course it was true," said Tibbs. "I wouldn't have written it otherwise."

"Just one moment, though," said the editor. "The fact remains that you didn't have a shred of evidence. And you shouldn't have written what you did when there wasn't any proof. You were wrong to do that. Let's hope it won't happen in the future."

Tibbs looked up. "In the future?" he asked.

"Yes. I do hope that you'll be able to return to the newspaper. Will you come back?"

"Oh, yes, with pleasure," said Tibbs.

"Good, that's all agreed on then. And Tibbs, before you go I just want to say that it seems a long time since you wrote anything about cats. I don't see why you shouldn't write about them from time to time. As long as it's not too often."

"Fine," said Tibbs.

As soon as the interview was over, the Newspaper Cat

slipped out of the window and hurried to the roof to give Minnie the news.

"Your human's back with the newspaper."

Minnie gave a sigh of relief.

"And now you'll be able to go back," said the cat.

"Go back? Where?"

"Well," said the Newspaper Cat, "your sister will want you back, won't she? Surely you'll be going back to your old home now?"

"I don't know," Minnie said, feeling very confused. "Who said so?"

"I heard it somewhere. I think one or two of the cats mentioned it. Haven't you spoken to your sister?"

"No," said Minnie.

"Then I expect she'll be coming soon. To fetch you."

"But I don't want to go," said Minnie. "I've got a human. And he needs me all the time. He won't be able to find any news without me."

"He doesn't need you anymore," said the Newspaper Cat. "He's changed so much. He isn't at all shy anymore. He can do anything he wants now. Haven't you noticed?"

"Yes," said Minnie. "It's true. He goes up to people and asks them anything he likes now. His anger with Elbow has given him courage. He's learned to Make an Effort."

On her way back to the attic, Minnie talked to the Scruffy Cat, who also mentioned her sister.

"Your sister asks if you'll go around and see her," said the Scruffy Cat. "I haven't spoken to her myself but the message was passed on to me. I'd go if I were you."

"Yes," Minnie said hesitantly.

"I hear she's found a medicine to cure you," said the Scruffy Cat. "That'll be a relief, won't it? Just think how wonderful it'll be to be a cat again. Or don't you think so?"

"I—er—I'm not sure anymore," said Minnie.

She found Tibbs in his living room, bubbling over with excitement.

"I've got my job back and my home back, too!" he cried. "We're going to celebrate with a big plate of fish." In his happiness he didn't notice how silent Minnie was. Quiet and thoughtful and not happy at all.

Chapter 17

Is She a Cat Again?

Tibbs was woken by a silky paw stroking his face.
It was Fluff.

Tibbs looked at his alarm clock. "Quarter past three in the morning . . . Why did you wake me up, Fluff? Go back to the bottom of the bed."

But Fluff mewed urgently.

"Are you trying to tell me something? You know I can't understand you. Go to Minnie. She'll be in her box."

But Fluff wouldn't stop and he carried on mewing until Tibbs got up.

Minnie wasn't in her box. She must be out on the roof then. It was already getting light. The kittens were playing in a corner and Fluff seemed to be calling him to the skylight in the kitchen.

"What's the matter? Do you want me to look outside?"

Tibbs stuck his head out of the window and looked out across the rooftops. Two cats were sitting nearby on a sloping roof. One was a beautiful big ginger cat with a white chest and white tip to her tail.

Tibbs leaned out further and the window squeaked. The ginger cat looked at him.

He was so startled that he almost lost his balance and had to grab hold of the windowsill. It was Minnie.

He knew those eyes so well. And it was Minnie's face too, but a proper cat's face this time.

He wanted to call out her name but he was struck dumb with shock. It only lasted for a moment or two. The ginger cat turned around and vanished behind a chimney.

The Scruffy Cat stayed where she was. Her tail was waving slightly and there was a mysterious look in her yellow eyes.

Tibbs went back to his room, feeling rather confused. He sat down on the sofa and began to bite his nails.

"It can't be," he said. "It's nonsense. Where on earth did I get that idea? She'll be back any moment, just as she was before."

Fluff was still twining around his legs, still trying to tell him something. Never before had he wanted to understand a cat so badly. Something was wrong. That much he knew.

"What are you trying to tell me, Fluff? Has she turned into a cat again?" And then he said, "Oh, what nonsense. I'm half asleep. I'll go back to bed."

He tried to go back to sleep but he couldn't. He lay and waited. Minnie usually came home just as it was getting light. Then she went straight into her box. But he was getting more and more uneasy. At last he got up and went to make a cup of coffee.

Six o'clock in the morning. And Minnie hadn't come home yet.

Tibbs went to see if her things were still there. Her washcloth and toothbrush and so on. They were all there. And her suitcase was standing in the corner. Luckily.

Luckily? Why luckily? If she *had* turned into a cat then

she wouldn't need a suitcase anymore.

I must be going mad. How did I get such a crazy idea into my head?

At a quarter past six there was a ring at the door.

It's her! She's come to the front door, Tibbs thought.

But it wasn't Minnie. It was Bibi who came up the stairs.

"I'm sorry to come around so early, Tibbs," she said. "But I've had such a fright. I looked out of my window this morning and I saw Minnie walking past."

"Yes," said Tibbs. "And?"

Bibi fell silent and gave him a desperate look.

"Go on, Bibi."

"She's a cat again," said Bibi. She sounded nervous. She was scared that Tibbs would laugh at her. But Tibbs was very serious indeed. Even though he did say, "Come on now, Bibi, what nonsense!" he said it without conviction.

"It's true, really it is," said Bibi.

"I think I've seen her too," said Tibbs. "I tried to call her but she ran away. Where could she be?"

"I think she's gone back to her old home," said Bibi. "To her own garden."

"And where's that?"

"On Queen's Road. She told me once that she came from Queen's Road. In a house with a lilac tree beside the terrace. That's where she lived when she was still a cat."

Fluff began to mew again.

"I can't understand him," said Bibi. "But I'm sure he's telling us that I'm right. What shall we do, Tibbs?"

"Nothing," said Tibbs. "What *can* we do?"

"Go there," said Bibi. "To Queen's Road. And see if she's there."

"What a stupid idea," said Tibbs.

But ten minutes later they were walking down the street together in the early morning light.

It was a long way and it took them some time to find Queen's Road. It was a narrow twisting street lined with white houses that had big front gardens.

"I can't see a ginger cat anywhere," said Tibbs. "And I can't see any lilacs either."

"It must be at the back," said Bibi. "I'll have a look in the back gardens. It's still early, no one's up yet."

It was very quiet in the street at this early hour. Birds were singing and blossom trembled in the breeze. Tibbs waited on the corner for Bibi to come back. A big garbage can stood in front of one of the houses. The house itself wasn't really a house but some sort of office. A sign on the gate read: *Institute for Biochemical Research.*

And then Tibbs remembered something that Minnie had told him. When she was a cat she had eaten something from a garbage can and after that she had changed. He had laughed at her then but now he began to wonder. Who knew what might happen with all these modern scientific developments. Perhaps they had thrown something away that hadn't worked out.

Bibi came back then.

"It must be that one," she said pointing at a house next to the Institute. "There's a lilac behind it. But I didn't see a cat. Perhaps she's gone inside. *Oh! Look!*"

Tibbs looked.

The ginger cat was standing in the front garden. She was looking straight toward them. And they could both see that she had Minnie's eyes.

But the awful thing was that the cat had a thrush in her mouth. A newly caught, fluttering, living thrush.

Bibi screamed and waved her arms. The cat instantly disappeared with the bird into the bushes behind the house.

"I'm going after her!" Bibi shouted, but Tibbs pulled her back.

"Don't!" he said. "The bird is probably wounded and half-dead. It'll be better to leave it alone."

They stayed by the hedge together. Minnie had vanished with her prey and Bibi began to cry.

"Don't cry," said Tibbs. "It's only natural. Cats are cats. And they catch birds."

"Minnie often used to look like that," said Bibi. "Whenever we were sitting in the park and a bird came near, she used to look just like that. I hated it. I used to shout 'Don't!' And she always felt so embarrassed. But she isn't embarrassed anymore. And that's why I'm crying."

Tibbs was only half listening. He was wondering whether he should ring the bell. He wanted to ask the people who lived in the house if their ginger cat had been missing recently.

But they wouldn't be up yet, he remembered. It was still so early. And anyway, what would happen then? They'd probably say yes, the cat had been away for a while but had now come back. What could he do about it?

"Come on, we'd better go," he said.

"Don't you want to take her back with you?" asked Bibi.

"No," said Tibbs. "She's someone else's cat. And I've still got eight others at home."

They went home, slowly, sadly.

It hadn't been a pretty sight—their own Minnie with a living bird in her jaws.

Chapter 18

The Ginger Sister

It was nighttime and pitch dark when Minnie met her sister on the roof of the Building Society.

The Baker's Cat had come to her and said, "Your sister's waiting for you. It's urgent. You must come at once."

Even before Minnie saw her sister she could smell the familiar scent of family, a dependable scent of Home. And so she said right away, "Sniff noses?"

"Certainly not," her sister said viciously. "Not until you're back to normal."

"I don't know if that'll ever happen."

"Oh yes, it'll happen all right. And tonight. The moment is here."

"Where?" asked Minnie.

"I mean that it can happen *now*. It couldn't before. And it can't later on. This is your last chance. So come with me now."

"To your house, you mean?"

"I mean to *our* house. To *our* garden."

Minnie looked up at the great sky above the rooftops. It seemed to be getting a little lighter in the east. She could

see her sister very clearly. She still didn't seem very friendly.

"You chased me away, don't forget," Minnie said. "You said that you didn't want to see me again. You were angry because I took a suitcase and some of the woman's clothes. But I couldn't leave just as I was."

"That's all forgotten and forgiven," her sister said quickly. "The woman didn't even notice they had gone. She has so many suitcases, after all, and so many clothes. You knew that, anyway."

"But what made you *really* angry was the fact that I wasn't a cat anymore. You chased me out of the garden."

"That was *then*," said her sister. "You can come back now."

"Just as I am?"

"Listen," her sister said. "Tonight you can be cured. Tonight or tomorrow morning at the latest."

"How can you be so certain?"

"You may have heard that I *almost* suffered in the same way as you," the sister said.

"Yes, Aunt Molly told me."

"It wasn't nearly as bad with me as it was with you. But I ate something from the garbage can too. And dreadful things started to happen. My whiskers disappeared and my tail grew smaller and smaller. And I got such strange feelings. I wanted to walk on my hind legs. And I wanted to take showers instead of washing myself properly with spit."

"And then?" asked Minnie.

"I was cured by a thrush," said her sister. "I ate a thrush. It was as simple as that. You know that they seldom come into our garden. They have only been there once. They usually avoid us. But I managed to catch one. And I got better right away. It cured me. I know that thrushes eat herbs that can help cure all kinds of illness. Yours too."

"And? Are there thrushes in the garden now?"

"Just for tonight. Perhaps they'll still be there in the early morning. That's why you must come right away. It's already beginning to get light."

Minnie stayed where she was and thought.

"Come on," said her sister. "Come home with me."

"But I've got a home here," said Minnie. "A home and a human . . ." She fell silent. The attic and the human now seemed so terribly far away. And so unimportant. The smell of her sister was so warm and *right*.

"Do you remember how we used to catch starlings in the garden together?" asked her sister. "You know how lovely our garden is in the spring. Think about the lilac, it's in bloom now. You can sit on the woman's lap and purr. You can do all the things that are cattish and normal. Look at you, you don't know if you're coming or going. You're shivering, you're cold. Come with me and you'll soon have your fur back again."

Minnie was indeed cold. It would be so wonderful to have fur again, she thought. To stretch out on the tiles in the sun with my thick ginger coat. And the bliss of washing yourself with one leg in the air, and then biting between the pads on your paws. The bliss of having claws again that you can draw in or out whenever you want. And to scratch a brand-new chair to your heart's content.

"I'll come with you," said Minnie. "But just wait a minute while—"

"No, I can't wait. The sun will be up soon. What do you want to do?"

"I just want—I thought—I must pack my case—and there's my washcloth and the—"

"What do you mean?" cried her sister. "You don't need those things anymore. What use is a suitcase to a cat?"

"I thought—perhaps I should take it back—or leave it somewhere—" Minnie stammered.

"Don't make things more complicated than they already are," her sister said grumpily.

"But surely I can say good-bye?"

"Say good-bye? To your human? Have you gone out of your mind? If you do that he'll stop you from going. He'll lock you up."

"Let me at least say good-bye to the Scruffy Cat," Minnie cried unhappily. "And explain to her what's happened. It's only four roofs further on."

"Wait here," the sister hissed. "*I'll* do it for you. Stay where you are. I'll go and look for the Scruffy Cat in the gutter on your roof."

[153]

She set off across the shadowy rooftops, passing Bibi's window as she went.

When she came back she said, "She sends her regards."

"The Scruffy Cat?"

"Well, not your human anyway," said her sister. "I saw him leaning out of his window and I got out of his way as soon as I could. Yes, of course, the Scruffy Cat. She sends her regards. She hopes that you'll come back and see her when you've got a tail again. She says that I look a lot like you!"

Now it was morning, and the sun was shining.

Minnie had been sitting for hours in a shed in the back garden of the house on Queen's Road. Beside the lawn mower. She was still shivering a little, more from excitement than the cold. But I'll soon have fur again, she thought. As soon as the cure has worked.

It wasn't working so far. Her sister hadn't been able to catch a thrush.

"Will you be much longer?" Minnie called through the half-open shed door. "The sun's out already."

"Yes, that's right, rush me!" her sister snapped. "It'll be a great help if you rush me, I *don't* think! I'll go and have a look in the front garden."

From the shed Minnie could see the back of the house where she had been born and where she had lived as a kitten.

Soon she would be able to go inside again and get a saucer of milk and be stroked. And when she started to purr no one would say, "Don't do that, Miss Minnie!"

She knew every tree and every bush in this garden. She had caught frogs on the lawn, and even a mole once. She had scratched up the earth in the flower bed. And dug holes among the begonias. She was beginning to feel more and more like a cat again. It was going to work, she felt certain of that. And very soon too.

Then she was startled by a terrible squealing noise.

Her ginger sister appeared. She had caught a thrush in the front garden. Tibbs and Bibi were standing by the hedge at that very moment but Minnie didn't know that, of course. Her sister came trotting triumphantly towards her.

She couldn't say anything because her mouth was full of thrush but Minnie could tell from the look in her sister's eyes that she was feeling very pleased with herself.

The bird squeaked and screamed and flapped helplessly in the sister's terrible mouth. For one brief moment, Minnie thought, Yummmmy!

But as soon as her ginger sister came close enough, Minnie gave her a fierce slap and shouted, "Let go!"

Her sister dropped the prey in astonishment. The thrush immediately flew away, very unsteadily at first and then straight upwards, soaring towards freedom.

"Well, now you've done it!" the ginger sister said quietly and menacingly.

"I—I'm sorry," said Minnie. She felt very embarrassed.

"That really *is* the last straw," her sister hissed angrily. "I've been running around all night for your benefit. *All* night. And why? Because it's your last chance and because you're my sister. I've used every last ounce of my strength and ingenuity to find you a thrush. And then, when at last I've managed to catch one, *look what happens!*"

"I—I couldn't help it," Minnie stammered. "I just wasn't thinking."

"You just weren't thinking? That's a fine thing to say!

After all that I've done for you, you slap the bird out of my mouth. *Ha!*"

"It happened before I realized what I was doing," Minnie wailed. "Isn't there another one? Didn't you say there were two of them?"

"You surely don't imagine that I'm going through all that again, do you?" The sister was now almost beside herself with rage. "Do you know what you are? You're a *human*, that's what you are! You're just like that human of mine. That human of *ours*, I should say, as she used to be your human too. She loves to eat chicken but, oh my, you should see the fuss she makes if *we* catch a bird. She soon whips the bird away from us. Don't you remember? Don't you remember how we used to go on about it when you lived here? You used to get so angry then. What a hypocrite, you used to say. *She* eats chicken but won't let us eat birds."

"I remember," said Minnie.

"Well then, why did you do it?"

"I don't know. I think I must have changed."

"You've changed all right," said the ginger sister. "Too much, if you ask me. You'll never be the same again. Anyway, I've had enough. You're not my sister anymore. Go away! Get out of my garden! And stay out. Don't ever let me catch you here again."

She spat at Minnie so fiercely that she ran off, deeper into the garden. And then through a gap in the hedge into the garden next door and on and on, through gardens and gardens and gardens, still hearing the screeching of her sister far behind her.

As she ran, she thought about what had happened.

But what *had* happened? She had always loved to hunt and catch birds. Why had she behaved so unnaturally? In such an uncattish way? Saving a bird's life—what an idiotic thing for a cat to do!

She tried hard to find an answer. I *felt* that the bird was in pain, she thought. I *felt* that the creature was afraid. But once you start to *feel* that sort of thing, then you are no longer a cat. Oh no. Cats have no sympathy at all for birds. I really do think my last chance has passed me by.

Chapter 19

This Time It Was Carlos

The weather began to change as Tibbs and Bibi made their way back to their own part of town. The wind rose, great clouds appeared, and it began to drizzle.

"Will you be in time for school?" asked Tibbs.

"Oh yes," said Bibi. "There's plenty of time yet."

When they reached Market Square, Tibbs said, "Let's get out of the rain for a while. On that bench under the trees where it's dry."

They sat down and sucked peppermints in silence, feeling a little sad.

Well, at least I've got my job back, thought Tibbs. And I don't have to find somewhere else to live. So everything's all right again. Except that I've lost my secretary. And there won't be a Cats' Press Agency from now on either. There'll be no more news from the cats. I'll have to look for stories all by myself. Will I be able to do it? Have I got the nerve to manage it all alone?

"Of course I can do it," he told himself firmly. "I'm not shy anymore. I'm not scared to ask anyone anything anymore. And it's a really good thing that I'll *have* to do it on my own now. So why don't I feel happy? Why don't I feel the slightest bit pleased?"

His thoughts turned to Miss Minnie. There was so much that I wanted to ask her. Before she became a cat again. And I didn't even thank her properly. Not once. All I ever did was scold her if she did something cattish. She didn't even get paid. Oh well, that's something she won't need anymore.

These thoughts didn't cheer him up one bit. A pair of gloves, that's all she got from me. And that was only because I thought she might scratch someone. If only she'd come back . . . I wouldn't be angry, however catlike she was. She could scratch as much as she liked. And purr too. And rub her head against my sleeve. I liked her best when she purred, Tibbs thought.

Suddenly they heard a dog barking right behind their bench.

It was an enormous Great Dane. He was standing under a tree, looking up into the branches and barking.

Without saying a word, Tibbs and Bibi jumped to their feet and went to have a look. The dog was barking furiously and jumping up at the trunk like a mad thing. Then he was called away by his human. "Carlos!" a voice called. "Carlos, come here!"

Tibbs and Bibi stood looking up into the tree. Rain dripped down on them from the leaves. And there, high in the branches, they saw a leg and a shoe.

At that moment a milk truck came around the corner into the square.

"Oh, I wonder if you'd mind giving me a hand?" Tibbs asked the milkman. "My secretary is up a tree. And she can't get down."

"Was she chased by a dog?" asked the milkman. "I knew

it. It's happened here before. Hang on, I'll park the milk truck right underneath."

Two minutes later, Minnie was standing on the ground again and the milkman was driving away. She was wet through and covered with leaves, but no one cared. Tibbs and Bibi were both laughing with relief and they each put an arm around her damp shoulders.

"How wonderful!" said Tibbs. "How marvelous! We must have been imagining it, after all. It wasn't true. How could we possibly have thought it was!"

"What wasn't true?" asked Minnie.

It was raining harder now and they were getting wetter and wetter but none of them noticed.

"We saw you early this morning, Miss Minnie," said Tibbs. "At least, we thought it was you."

"A ginger cat," said Bibi. "I saw her on the roof first."

"It was my sister," said Minnie. "My quin-sister. She looks just like me."

"And then again on Queen's Road," said Tibbs. "We went there. And we saw that cat again. With a thrush."

"Yes, that was her too. My sister."

"But we're getting soaked!" Tibbs cried. "Come on, let's go home."

And when he said "Let's go home," he felt so happy that he wanted to burst out singing at the top of his voice, there in the street in the rain.

"*I* can't come, I've got to go to school," said Bibi miserably. "And so I'll never hear what happened."

"Come on over when school is finished," said Minnie. "And I'll tell you the whole story all over again."

Dripping wet, Tibbs and Minnie made their way back to the attic where all the cats were waiting for them. The Scruffy Cat and Fluff and the kittens all crowded around them, purring and mewing.

"We'd better get into some dry clothes," said Tibbs. "And then you can tell me everything."

Minnie told him everything that had happened. About her sister. And why she had run away.

"I wanted to be a cat again so much," she said. "At least, that's what I thought. But when it came down to it, I just couldn't. I just wasn't sure."

"And are you sure now?" Tibbs asked.

"I think so," said Minnie. "I'm quite certain now. I would much rather be a human. But I'm scared that I might still behave like a cat sometimes. After all, I climbed into a tree

[161]

again just now. When that dog came along."

"It doesn't matter," said Tibbs.

"And I've noticed that I still purr."

"You can do it as much as you like," said Tibbs. "Purr and scratch and rub your head against people."

"I don't feel like scratching anything at the moment," said Minnie. "But it would be nice to rub my head against you . . ."

"Go right ahead," said Tibbs.

Minnie rubbed her head against his sleeve. A very wet head because her ginger hair wasn't yet dry.

"I was so scared," Tibbs stammered. "I was so scared that I'd never see you again, Miss Minnie. I felt really terrible when I found out that you'd gone. Never run away again. Will you promise me that?"

"I'll never run away again," said Minnie. "But *I* was scared that you didn't need me anymore. All your shyness has gone."

"I need you a great deal, Minnie," said Tibbs. "And not just as a secretary." He went very red. "I need you here in the house, near me, do you know what I mean, Minnie?"

He realized that he had stopped calling her "Miss Minnie" and looked shyly away. And until now she had always been careful to call him "Mr. Tibbs." But now she smiled at him and said, "I'd really love some breakfast, Tibbs. A whole tin of sardines. And then I must go out onto the roof. The Scruffy Cat wants to talk to me in private."

"Well, go and do that first," said Tibbs. "And then I'll make us all a big breakfast with all sorts of nice things to eat." He went into the kitchen and Minnie went out of the window onto the roof, followed by the Scruffy Cat.

"Something's the matter," Minnie said. "What is it? It

[162]

looks as though you aren't very happy to see me back."

"Of course I'm glad you've come back," said the Scruffy Cat. "It's not that at all. It's just—well, look, I just don't have any respect for you anymore. I'm sorry, but that's how it is. It seems to me that it's all gone a little too far."

"What, that I've come back?"

"No, I mean that story about the thrush and your sister. I've seen a great deal during my time as a stray cat but never anything like that. Feeling sorry for a thrush, indeed! The very thought of it makes me feel sick! You'll be feeling sorry for fish next. Before we know where we are you'll be going to the fishseller and grabbing the herring out of his paws—I mean, hands. Forgive me for talking like this but I'm rather upset about it."

"Yes, you *are* being rather rude," said Minnie.

"And I just want to let you know that I'll be on my way again soon," said the Scruffy Cat. "My children are eating from a dish now. You can find homes for them if you like. They don't need me anymore. Oh yes, I've got some more news for you. I've just heard it from the Deodorant Cat. The extension to the deodorant factory won't be going ahead. The Council won't give their permission. Pass the news on to your human."

"Thank you," said Minnie.

"I suppose the Cats' Press Agency will be carrying on as usual?" asked the Scruffy Cat.

"Of course. Everything will be just as it was before."

"And you'll still go into your box?" asked the Scruffy Cat. "To sleep?"

"Of course," said Minnie. "Why not?"

"Oh, I don't know." The Scruffy Cat stared at her suspiciously with her yellow eyes. She was looking very grubby

[163]

and bedraggled again. "Do you know what?" she said softly. "I've got a funny feeling that you're going to marry him."

"What on earth gave you that idea?" asked Minnie.

"Oh, it's just a feeling that I've got," said the Scruffy Cat. "But I must warn you. If you do that, then your last chance will have gone forever. You'll never be a cat again. And there may come a time when you won't be able to talk to us anymore. When you won't be able to understand what we say. And you'll even forget the Miaow-Miaow Song."

"Well, it hasn't happened yet," said Minnie.

Tibbs stuck his head out of the kitchen window and called, "Breakfast is ready! For cats *and* people!"

"Come on then," said Minnie. "Let's go inside."